Carlisle's Molly Pitcher

Mary Ludwig Hays McCauley

J. M. West

LOCAL HISTORY PRESS

an imprint of Sunbury Press, Inc.
Mechanicsburg, PA USA

LOCAL HISTORY
PRESS

an imprint of Sunbury Press, Inc.
Mechanicsburg, PA USA

Copyright © 2024 by J. M. West.
Cover Copyright © 2024 by Sunbury Press, Inc.

For information about special discounts for bulk purchases, please contact Sunbury Press Orders Dept. at (855) 338-8359 or orders@sunburypress.com.

To request one of our authors for speaking engagements or book signings, please contact Sunbury Press Publicity Dept. at publicity@sunburypress.com.

FIRST LOCAL HISTORY PRESS EDITION: September 2024

Set in Adobe Garamond Pro | Interior design by Crystal Devine | Cover by Lawrence Knorr | Edited by Lawrence Knorr.

Publisher's Cataloging-in-Publication Data
Names: West, J. M., author.
Title: Carlisle's Molly Pitcher : Mary Ludwig Hays McCauley / J. M. West.
Description: First trade paperback edition. | Mechanicsburg, PA : Local History Press, 2024.
Summary: A fictionalized account of Mary Ludwig Hays McCauley's life story, the most plausible "Molly Pitcher" from the American Revolution, based on the historical record.
Identifiers: ISBN : 979-8-88819-217-7 (softcover).
Subjects: FICTION / Historical / Colonial America & Revolution | FICTION / Women | FICTION / War & Military.

Designed in the USA
0 1 1 2 3 5 8 13 21 34 55

For the Love of Books!

Contents

Preface

Who was Molly Pitcher? A symbol of all the brave women who helped in countless untold ways to win the Revolutionary War? A blend of anonymous or autonomous women who left their homes to become soldiers? What prompted these women to rebel against social constraints? Were they also passionate about freedom? From woman to legend to myth, why did fame favor Molly Pitcher or Mary Ludwig in Carlisle's case?

Wives, mothers, and sisters who followed their men felt safer than staying at home because they felt vulnerable. Several cut their hair and wore men's uniforms to fight as men. Indeed, many were willing to battle for freedom. History does not record every woman's story. Soldiers seemed surprised to find women on the battlefield, except for ones who carried water, bound wounds or offered food or comfort. Still others remained anonymous.

Why the mystery and debate over Molly Pitcher?

Soldiers on the battlefield needed water for themselves, their horses, and the cannons, especially during battles and skirmishes. They called out, "Molly, pitcher," and "Molly" hurried to quench their thirst. In time, Molly became a nickname for Mary, a popular name during the 1700s.

People have debated whether Mary Ludwig Hays is *the* "Molly Pitcher," as if only one or no woman achieved that distinction. Because of the compelling evidence, most historians accept that Mary Ludwig Hays fought in battle. "At Fort Clinton, she fired the last shot before the fortress fell, and the pivotal Battle of Monmouth[1] "Molly Pitcher" symbolized one of the Revolutionary War's iconic hero- ines. However, women's valiant efforts on the battlefield were a scandalous anomaly at the time. In Carlisle, she would find like-minded souls.

Centrally located, Carlisle, the county seat, grew pros- perous as a gateway to the west and the staging area for the army. From the west, fur traders and Indians traveled to the town to trade pelts for food, guns, and domestic goods. It also became the residence of a fifteen-year-old domestic.

Born in Trenton, New Jersey, on October 23, 1754, the daughter of Maria Margaretha and John G. Ludwig. Mary Ludwig moved to the borough of Carlisle to Dr. and Anna Irvine's residence at age fifteen. She had a brother, Johann, who joined the war effort. Sources differ on the number of other siblings she may have had. Mrs. Anna Irvine spotted Ludwig doing her chores. Irvine employed Mary as a maid and housekeeper for eight years to assist their growing family. During Ludwig's first year in Carlisle, she married John Casper Hays in 1769,[2] a barber in town. Joining her husband at Valley Forge, Hays became a "camp follower."

Camp followers were wives, mothers with children, sisters, and prostitutes who trailed behind both British and Continental Armies carrying their belongings. Women had good reasons to avoid British Regulars (army); they feared the Redcoats would attack, ransack their homes, steal their food, and rape them. They felt

1. Benson Bobrick, *Angel in the Whirlwind: The Triumph of the American Revolution* (New York: Penguin Books, 1997), 346.

2. Stephanie Bearce, *The American Revolution: Spies, Secret Missions, and Hidden Facts* (Waco, Texas: Prufrock Press, 2015), 59.

safer and could care for their men if they traveled with them. Their efforts helped the Continentals win the war, though their presence embarrassed General Washington and other officers. They felt the followers were dirty, noisy, and distracting, but one of his generals reminded his leader that camp followers worked hard, helped the cause, and boosted morale.

A day in the life of a camp follower meant rising at daybreak to light fires and adding logs to keep embers burning throughout the night. Then, women fixed breakfast, usually porridge (oats) and tea or coffee. They cooked, did laundry, carried messages, mended uniforms, and nursed the ill[3] while on the road. They also made bandages to dress wounds. Women and older children foraged for food and built lean-tos, or a few lucky ones pitched tents provided by the army. For them, danger lurked everywhere.

Scouting for pockets of the Redcoats, tribal enemies, or wild animals meant being constantly alert. They avoided cities where the British had installed soldiers. At best, British soldiers often treated colonists with disdain; at worst, Redcoats stole animals, food, weapons, and ammunition. They destroyed occupied homes and ransacked cities. Some native tribes raided settlements and killed occupants to stem European migration. Other tribes fought with Great Britain because King George III had declared land beyond the Appalachian Mountains the boundary for white settlement.

When newly recruited soldiers set up camp at Valley Forge (1777), camp followers fed them, too. Women with children had an added burden: keeping youngsters fed, clothed, sheltered, and safe, never mind clean. Packing and

---

3. Ibid., 9.

unpacking also took time. Days of camping and following the army seemed endless because most camp followers lacked adequate transportation; most walked hundreds of miles carrying their provisions. Washington's men and followers traveled over one hundred miles over rugged terrain from Valley Forge to the courthouse for the Monmouth Battle.

In June 1778, at Monmouth Courthouse, when the temperature rose to 100+ degrees, Ludwig-Hays took water to the soldiers in her husband's regiment; she also fought bravely at the Battle at the Monmouth Courthouse. Several eye-witnesses put Ludwig-Hays on the battlefield manning a cannon. In time, Pennsylvania recognized her efforts, awarding her an annual pension for "services rendered." 'Sergeant Molly,' the soldiers called her.[4]

Others claim that the title belongs to Margaret Corbin. Born in Franklin County, Pennsylvania, on November 11, 1751, relatives reared her after Indians killed her father and captured her mother. She eventually moved to York, where she married John Corbin. Margaret Corbin was severely wounded in the arm during the battle of Ft. Washington in 1776 in Manhattan. Soldiers in Corbin's unit nicknamed her "Captain Molly" and "Dirty Kate." Disabled, Corbin sought a pension from the state. After her injury, the army moved her to West Point on "Invalid Detail," where she completed simple tasks like rolling bandages.[5] By the time of the Battle of Monmouth in Freehold, New Jersey, she was permanently disabled. In 1779, Pennsylvania honored Corbin, 'the first woman

---

4. John Landis, *A Short History of Molly Pitcher, The Heroine of the Battle of Monmouth* (Carlisle, Pa.: The Corman Print Co., 1905), 13–14.

5. "Margaret Corbin," accessed at: https://en.wikipedia.org/wiki/Margaret_Corbin.

soldier,' *with* an annual fifty-dollar pension for fighting in the Revolutionary War.[6]

The couples shared a few traits. Both husbands were named John. Corbin and Hays first served in Proctor's artillery. Prior to the war, both couples lived in Pennsylvania. Both women took their husband's positions as cannons during battle. Mary and Margaret shared similar names, and the nickname Molly was a common choice. Each woman received a pension for her service.

However, the women's backgrounds differed: Margaret Corbin wore a soldier's uniform; Mary Hays wore her clothes. Corbin and Hays also had different nicknames, birthdates, hometowns, burial sites, and death dates.

After the Monmouth Courthouse battle, the Hayes returned home to Carlisle. After her husband died in 1786, Mary remarried—John McCauley, an artilleryman who fought with her husband. Later, she suffered an eye injury but continued to work, minding children, mending clothes, and cleaning Carlisle's public buildings.[7]

Confusing Hays and Corbin's stories does neither woman justice.

Several sources state the nickname "Molly Pitcher" did not appear until the early 1800s. However, witnesses at Monmouth Courthouse, relatives, and Carlisle neighbors testified knowing of Ludwig Hays McCauley. A local paper at the time printed a poem about 'Molly Pitcher,' referring to Ludwig-Hays,[8] but she wasn't the only female soldier.

---

6. Ibid.

7. John Landis, *A Short History of Molly Pitcher, The Heroine of the Battle of Monmouth* (Carlisle, Pa.: The Corman Print Co., 1905), 17.

8. "Margaret Corbin," accessed at: https://en.wikipedia.org/wiki/Margaret_Corbin.

Thousands of women risked their lives working as spies, couriers, and signalers during the War of Independence. Other women like Deborah Sampson and Annie Maria Lane fought in the American Revolution. A South Carolina native, Sally St. Clair, died fighting during the siege of Savannah in 1779.[9] They deserve recognition, too. This book, though, depicts the exploits of Carlisle's Molly Pitcher after moving to town to work for Dr. and Mrs. Irvine.

---

9. Ibid.

Author's Note

For my purposes, this book follows Carlisle's Mary Ludwig Hays McCauley's timeline, which limits content and others' commentary of this determined soldier who demonstrates a woman's strength to live by her standards rather than those delineated for women in the eighteenth century. By limiting the narrative, I've omitted thousands of men, women, and children who contributed to the Revolutionary War in myriad ways, especially soldiers on the Monmouth battlefield, a turning point in the war.

To that end, I've provided a thumbnail sketch of Colonial Carlisle for the readers to situate themselves in the context of the time leading up to Mary Ludwig Hays McCauley's life and her particular contribution to winning America's independence from Great Britain, specifically from 1769 to 1782.

COLONIAL CARLISLE—THE BEGINNING

In 1681, English King Charles II granted Quaker William Penn 80,000 acres to repay a debt. Penn provided a haven for people persecuted for their religious beliefs in their native countries. Penn's Woods, or Pennsylvania, one of the 'middle colonies' of the original thirteen, drew people of all religions. Independent-minded Scots-Irish flocked to the Carlisle area. Quakers, Germans, and many Pennsylvania Dutch, Presbyterians, and Anabaptists sought the right to worship without fear of retaliation.

Anglicans—British citizens (Church of England) also put down roots here. Others arrived on the Atlantic shore for economic reasons. Numerous Europeans who couldn't afford passage to the New World indentured themselves and their relatives to pay off their debt. Still, others pushed west from the Atlantic coastal cities to this frontier town to build better lives for their families in the 'new world.' Since the *Mayflower* landed on Plymouth Rock, the pilgrims considered America the "new" England, a shining beacon on the hill, a covenant with God for a new beginning where men could own land and prosper by hard work and perseverance.

Landowners enjoyed privileges like shaping, developing, and controlling Carlisle's growth. Businessmen and landowners like Penn were called Proprietors; this title and his appointees, including his youngest son, Thomas, referred to local leaders who eventually became civic-minded guardians of colonial towns.

Thomas Penn hired a surveyor to find a central, southeastern town with a continuous water supply. Thomas Holme or John Armstrong Sr. recommended three places; the colonial governor, James Hamilton, chose the site near Letort Spring, named after the man with a trading post at the spring's head. Penn's youngest son, Thomas, established Carlisle in 1751. Carlisle was an interior town because it was centrally located. Letort Spring provided water; roads and Indian paths radiated in all directions like wagon wheel spokes. Penn laid the town out in a grid pattern, with Hanover and High Street intersecting at the square, similar to many other colonial towns.

As proprietors, Penn and Thomas wanted "to control commerce and [the] land, to secure a common border"[10] from North Mountain to South Mountain, which also contained the Yellow Breeches Creek. By 1765, "Carlisle had townspeople who had 26 servants, 21 slaves, and others [who] served as domestics,"[11] including Mary Ludwig. These men had the power to sell a plot or lease a hundred acres to homesteaders. They could also revoke the contract if the settlers failed to meet the criteria: build a permanent dwelling on the land, till at least five acres and live on site for twelve consecutive years. 'Control' also meant political. As early as 1744, Carlisle's leaders declared their opposition to British taxation, interference with the colony's business, and the king and Parliament's attitude toward the colonies.

Most towns contained general stores, schools, and churches; some had paved roads. Carlisle boasted "a wheelwright, two saddlers, a shoemaker, tailor, weaver, carpenter, cooper (barrel-makers), feltmaker, brewer, two hatters, three bricklayers, and two silversmiths."[12] White-washers, unskilled laborers, innkeepers, and transients traveled through the town going west or settled down to farm, open a trade, or operate a business. A nearby quarry supplied tons of limestone for building.

Chosen as the county seat, Carlisle residents were required to build a rudimentary goal (jail), Quaker and Presbyterian meeting houses, a pillory, and a courthouse on the square. Local citizens did not make the town's market house until the following century because settlers

---

10. Judith Ridner, *A Town In-between: Carlisle, Pennsylvania, and the Early Mid-Atlantic Interior* (Philadelphia: University of Pennsylvania Press, 2010), 21.

11. Ibid., 27.

12. Ibid., 53.

had to construct their houses and churches first. Building structures, infrastructure, and travelers created noise. Businesses mushroomed; opportunities for growth and urban development increased as the town encompassed both rich and poor, both solid and sordid citizens. Distinct social classes emerged, including a growing middle class of tradesmen and business owners.

According to the Crown's 1736 treaty provision, white settlers could not inhabit land farther west than the Appalachian Mountains. The chiefs claimed that squatters had built cabins on their land.[13] In 1750, provincial authorities led by Richard Peters and Conrad Weiser removed the mostly Scots-Irish squatters in an incident known as "Burnt Cabins." Today, this village is still known by that name.

In 1753, the Six Nations (Mohawk, Oneida, Seneca, Onondaga, Tuscarora, and Cayuga) proposed that Governor Hamilton meet with chiefs in Carlisle to create permanent boundaries between Carlisle and the Ohio Valley. He agreed but didn't attend; he sent representatives, including Ben Franklin, to that meeting to settle the dispute. While the meeting opened a dialogue between Carlisle settlers and the indigenous people, the summit failed to stop the waves of expansion.

Like most frontier towns, Carlisle had opponents and supporters among the Native American tribes, whom settlers pushed ever westward.[14] The Susquehannock and Delaware called Pennsylvania their home until European immigrants and westward expansion pushed them out.

---

13. Robert Secor, ed., *Pennsylvania 1776* (University Park, Pa.: Pennsylvania State University Press, 1975), 154–55.

14. Ibid., 22.

Some of the tribes retaliated with brutal attacks and raids
on settlers. Members of the Pennsylvania militia led by
surveyor Colonel John Armstrong, whose brother had
been murdered by natives in the weeks prior, attacked the
warriors at Kittanning with mixed results.

Armstrong returned home a hero and was honored with
a medal because settlers along the frontier were relieved
that the Kittanning battle halted Indian raids temporarily,
but later, historians said he did not achieve his goal of
destroying the camp. Thus, fear of retaliation weighed
heavily on settlers' minds.[15] The proximity of the hostile
tribes (Susquehannock, Cherokee, and Catawba) kept the
local citizens alert and watchful. Town leaders like fur and
skin trader Robert Callender, lawyer James Wilson, John
Armstrong, and wealthy store owner and soldier John
Montgomery joined the state militia as officers, who also
delved into local politics.[16]

Indian tribes that aided Carlisle residents included
the Shawnee and Tuscarora, who built multi-tribal,
permanent settlements in the Susquehanna Valley. Their
numbers had been decimated by European diseases soon
after contact, followed by brutal battles among themselves
and with the colonial militia. Once the colonials pushed
westward, many tribes rebelled against white settlers who
squatted on their lands in the Susquehanna Valley.

During the Colonial Era, large families were necessary.
"The children worked alongside their parents, helping
with gardens in the spring, haymaking in summer,
pressing cider, husking corn, and gathering nuts in the

15. D. W. Thompson and Merri Lou Schaumann, "Goodbye Molly Pitcher," *Cumberland County History*, 1989 Summer, Volume 6, Number 1.

16. Judith Ridner, *A Town In-between: Carlisle, Pennsylvania, and the Early Mid-Atlantic Interior* (Philadelphia: University of Pennsylvania Press, 2010), 78.

fall."[17] They milked the cows by hand and helped with the animals. Even youngsters fed chickens and gathered eggs. Harvest celebrations capped the growing season throughout the colonies as devout citizens thanked God and friendly Native Americans for their blessings. As expected, boys usually helped their fathers; girls, their mothers.

At about age thirteen, boys usually were apprenticed to a tradesman for seven years without pay or until they set up their shop. Male children usually followed in their father's footsteps on farms since agriculture dominated the rural areas. Girls learned domestic skills like sewing, weaving, carding, and spinning wool. Mothers taught daughters culinary skills like cooking in a cauldron in the fireplace, churning butter, and watching younger siblings—every day a challenge for survival.

Daughters of the landed gentry and the well-to-do in cities learned to sew, play the piano, and study comportment or etiquette. Their brothers attended college or studied abroad. When time permitted, children played. Girls enjoyed having cornhusks or rag dolls; boys received toy soldiers or carved animals and weapons. Children also played games like Blind Man's Bluff as time permitted, but commoners struggled.[18]

In wealthy cities like Philadelphia, however, citizens enjoyed the materials imported from Europe: "the finest satins, silk, laces. In five or six courses, bountiful food like ham, beef, mutton, pork, lamb, scrapple . . . wild game" and fish graced their dining tables. They had various drinks: "tea, coffee, wine, whiskey, Madeira, claret, rum

17. Joshua J. Mark, "Daily Life in Colonial America," *World History Encyclopedia* accessed at https://www.worldhistory.org/article/1722/daily-life-in-colonial-america/.

18. Robert Secor, ed., *Pennsylvania 1776* (University Park, Pa.: Pennsylvania State University Press, 1975), 154–55.

punch, and chocolate"[19]—plus cider and milk. Citizens
entertained and mingled with British officers. Servants
and some enslaved people served the wealthy residents.

Imagine a wilderness where few stores offered ready-
made goods. Frontier settlers made nearly everything:
cabins, clothes, quilts, shoes, furniture, pewter dishes,
rugs, tools, ammunition, and rifles. Cannons, wagons,
harnesses, horseshoes, and plows required extensive time
and effort. Before the Revolution, colonists imported quill
pens, ink, paper, books, and candles from England.

Settlers felled trees, cleared areas, and built cabins.
In Carlisle, commoners built small crude cabins with
paper-covered windows and dirt floors, one or two
rooms, and a loft for sleeping. Cabin dwellers chinked
the gaps with mud and straw. The fireplace provided heat
and a cooking source. Others less fortunate dug holes
into the hills and covered the roof with moss. Two-story
farmhouses dotted rural Cumberland County. Few roads
existed, but Indian trails, which fanned out in five directions, offered a blueprint for road building.

Yet a looming discontent wafted across the land.

As early as 1754, conflicts of interest divided colonists
who favored freedom, while Loyalist city dwellers wanted
British protection from the Indians, carpetbaggers, and
criminals. Along the western frontier, French fur trappers
and traders had been bartering with the natives for a
century and resented British rulers imposing burdensome
taxes. Carlisle was a critical transit point during the
French and Indian War, especially following Braddock's

---

19. Judith Ridner, *A Town In-between: Carlisle, Pennsylvania, and the Early Mid-At-lantic Interior* (Philadelphia: University of Pennsylvania Press, 2010), 115.

Defeat, making its citizens keenly aware and fearful of the enemies on their western border if the world's best army could not subdue them.

In 1763, Dr. William Irvine and his wife Anna Callender, Robert's daughter, moved to Carlisle, bought a corner lot where the Presbyterian Church now stands, built a large house, and became leading citizens.

As in other colonial towns, Carlisle residents opposed the Stamp Act, which taxed paper products like letters, wills, diaries, stationery, ink and pens, and other related products. In 1768, the Irvines hired a domestic named Mary Ludwig.[20]

In 1773, due to the colonists' rising ire, the Sons of Liberty, allegedly led by Samuel Adams, visited Boston Harbor disguised as Indians. The disguised Sons tossed one hundred crates of tea into the sea—the famous Boston Tea Party. England punished the rebels by closing Boston's port and appointing Loyalists as governors. These punishing policies, in part, spurred the rebellion.

Guild members considered the Intolerable Acts, the Coercive Acts by Parliament, especially egregious because they punished Boston for the Sons of Liberty's actions. Limiting Massachusetts's individual and state rights, imposing punitive taxes, and appointing British governors amounted to "taxation without representation." In Carlisle, the result prompted its leaders to meet and submit seven resolutions colonies could take, including boycotting British goods.[21]

With the publication of the Declaration of Independence, colonials had to decide whether to support the

20. John Landis, *A Short History of Molly Pitcher, The Heroine of the Battle of Monmouth* (Carlisle, Pa.: The Corman Print Co., 1905), 24.

21. Ibid, 10.

Continental Army or accept British rule. Violence erupted between the Loyalists and Patriots, who often cast the Crown's governors and appointees out of their houses. These Loyalists were tarred and feathered and run out of town. Rebels met in secret to shore up supplies, plan a defense, and hide their valuables, including animals, from marauding British soldiers. Settlers with money, however, were better suited to plotting clandestine activities against what they considered British aggression.

When the conflict escalated, Dr. Irvine joined the army as a brigadier general.

1

Mary Ludwig Hays

After bidding her parents farewell, the girl clopped down the lane to the hard-packed dirt trail; Mary Ludwig stood waiting for her future. The fifteen-year-old was moving from Trenton, New Jersey, to work in Carlisle, Pennsylvania. Her meager belongings—an everyday skirt and muslin blouse, petticoats, her Sunday outfit, comb, and hairbrush fit in a worn valise. A ruffled white cap covered her cropped, wavy brown hair. She wore a blue and white short skirt, petticoat, [white blouse], a fitted blue jacket, a broad white cap with flaring ruffles, sun bonnet, woolen stockings, and . . . brogans.[22] Her Mother packed her daughter's lunch in butcher's paper.

As the sun climbed higher, Mrs. Anna Irvine's horses arrived. Ludwig packed her food staples into the saddle bags. Tossed the saddlebags behind her rolled blanket. Over the saddle horn, she looped her valise and heaved herself into the saddle. Mrs. Irvine clucked to the horses. The hundred and twenty-five miles to Carlisle allowed Irvine and Ludwig time to get to know each other.

---

22. Ibid., 9.

"Tell me about yourself," Mrs. Irvine invited. "I've convinced your parents to let you come home to work for us. I saw you from the neighbor's working hard at your chores."

Mary shrugged. "Ain't much to tell. I never went to school. Trenton is as far as I've traveled. Papa has enough hands to help milk cows and run the butcher shop, so my parents told me I'm going into service."

"Well, schooling is more important for men. They have to support a family," Mrs. Irvine replied. "Are you willing to work for us? Can you sew?"

"Yes'm. I like to keep busy. I made this skirt." Mary plucked at the striped calico. "I can clean, cook, run errands, and mind children. And I knit and chop wood. I've churned butter and made tallow candles. I'm willing to try 'bout anything. How about yourself?"

Mrs. Irvine's eyebrows arched. "Well, I hope you won't need to chop wood! You can help make beeswax candles. You are currently our only live-in domestic. As for myself, I grew up on a farm in Mercer County.[23] I like the frontier. Later, we moved to town. Carlisle is cleaner and quieter than bigger towns." Mrs. Irvine laid a hand across her stomach. "I managed most wifely duties myself, but now that I am with child, I will need your help."

"Oh, a baby." Mary smiled. "When's the baby due?"

"In January, if I counted correctly." She beamed. They forded a stream so the horses could drink. "We'll stop here for lunch."

"Yes, it's beautiful—all the colorful trees." The maples were dressed in yellow, scarlet, and rust. The wind wrestled elm leaves from trees; they scattered, mimicking the

---

23. "Dr. William Irvine," accessed at www.irvineclan.com.

cardinals and wrens. Dried hickory leaves held on, but nuts pelted to the ground. The mighty oaks stood thick and tall as the last to lose their leaves. Ferns, scrub trees, wild berry bushes, a cushion of White pine needles, and rotting logs sprouting moss comprised the forest's thick undergrowth. The women hobbled the horses; in a sunny spot, they dusted off a solid log and sat down to enjoy their repast.

Mrs. Irvine continued, "We will provide room, board, and a monthly wage. After church, you'll have Sundays off." She patted her lips with a cloth napkin, shook it out, and tucked it in the reticule around her waist.

Mary thought it rude to ask 'How much?" but she would send some money home.

2

Meeting Carlisle

Dr. William and Mrs. Anna Irvine's limestone mansion sat on a spacious corner lot on North Bedford and North Streets. Leaves dropped golden puddles beneath trees. Dusty and tired from the ride, the women fed, watered the horses and rubbed them down. At dusk, they hustled into the house. Opening the massive front door with a skeleton key, Mrs. Irvine gestured for Mary to follow.

Mrs. Irvine ushered Mary into the grand house; "Well, here we are. Let's see what Cook made us for dinner. Let's eat dinner."

Their chicken dinner rested on pewter plates, still warm, on the Franklin stove. They ate in the dining room. Mary's eyes roamed over the flocked wallpaper, wainscoting, and China closet. Drawn velvet curtains hid tall windows. Beyond the foyer lay the drawing room opposite the living room, all with fireplaces.

Anna continued. "I'll show you around and explain your responsibilities like cleaning, laundry, and helping with the baby. You can also weed the kitchen garden; we must dig up the potatoes, carrots, and turnips soon. We're getting low on candles; the wax and wicks are in the back closet with the garden tools. We store wood ashes in that cast iron pot for the lye soap.

As she talked, Mrs. Irvine glided along the hardwood floors, showing Mary where she stored the cleaning implements. "Can you card and spin wool?"

"Yes'm, and quilt too."

Mrs. Irvine showed Mary how to polish the silverware, iron, and press linens.

At the back door, hooks held several straw hats and two worn coats with boots below. "You may use this sun bonnet and these garden gloves."

"Dr. Irvine informed me last night that he'd be late coming home. He has a meeting in town. Since Dr. Irvine emigrated from Ireland, he's fond of Irish foods. He is a physician—but going at all hours, so you may need to help patients when they pick up their tinctures and drugs."

"Yes, ma'am." Mary nodded.

Dr. Irvine's office had tall, spacious windows. A quill, inkstand, and broadsheets lay on his large desk; his chair was tucked neatly underneath. Leather-bound books lined the shelves on the wall behind his desk. Two armchairs flanked the fireplace on the other side of the room.

A stairway led upstairs. A canopy topped the couple's double bed in the first bedroom with an armoire close beside. A sitting area snuggled in front of the window with a rocking chair and a bassinet alongside. As befitting Dr. Irvine's station, various powdered wigs waited on their stands for the doctor when attending formal occasions or going out in public. Other bedrooms held single beds, dressers, and side tables bearing hurricane lamps. Pitchers and basins perched on wood stands. Hooked rugs partially covered the hardwood floors. A harvest moon threw lacy patterns against the opposite wall. Anna moved toward the window and drew the shutters and curtains for the night.

Mrs. Irvine showed Mary her room with a tiny window at the end of the hall. A single bed occupied one corner. An armoire for clothes stood against the outside wall. On the top shelf sat a felt hat for church. A washstand held a basin and pitcher with clean cloths below. "Any questions?"

"No, ma'am. Thank you for the hat." Mary stared at the polished hardwood and the ornate furniture. "Your house is mighty purty. It's nothing like our house on the farm." The Irvine house smelled like roasted meat, linseed oil, and lemons, whereas the Ludwig home smelled of sauerkraut, sweat, and sunshine. On the farm, the odor of cow dung stung the air year around, and the chickens scolded like magpies when she scattered their feed.

Behind the mansion, a fireplace served as an outdoor kitchen. Yards away, a black kettle sat over a fire pit for washdays. A slate path led to the outhouse beside a crib with dry corn cobs visible under a covered lean-to. Climbing ivy partially hid the wooden structure from view.

On sunny fall days, Mary rambled down the streets of Carlisle, the quiet and quaint county seat. The courthouse, a few shops including the cobbler, tailor, barber, hatter, a general store, churches, and houses lined Main Street. Fort Lowther, hardly more than a stockade, dominated the middle of town. At the cobbler's, Mary noticed short, stout boots ideal for the upcoming winter. On another day, she discovered a sparkling stream at the west end of town. Wild raspberry tubers bent over the water. Tall grasses, slender trees, and weeds crowded its banks.

At the Irvine house, life fell into a routine. After a quick breakfast, Mary washed the breakfast dishes. She emptied the chamber pots into the outhouse and beat the rugs outside. Then she opened the curtains and made beds. After snuffing out the embers in the bedroom fire-places, she shoveled the ashes into a bucket, carried them out, and dumped them under the laundry cauldron.

After lunch, Hays returned to her work. Mixing linseed oil and turpentine made fine wood polish for the furniture, stairway banister, and all the dark furniture. She worked her way downstairs, humming as she dusted.

Later in the day, Mrs. Irvine showed her how to make Irish Brown Bread, 'bangers and mash,' and other Irish recipes Dr. Irvine liked. "And the doctor is deeply involved in politics at this unsettled time." Mrs. Irvine said.

"Hmm. Looks like people are choosing sides," Mary commented. "Some Colonists in Trenton resent the Red-coats' presence, but most living in the city are Loyalists. They don't seem to mind the Brits occupying their homes or eating their food. Can't imagine city livin'. All manner of people crowded together like that. Here, it seems like people are getting angry at the Motherland. Why's that?"

Anna agreed. "Yes. More's the pity. England has allowed us the freedom to do as we please, but now the Crown is trying to rein us in. Britain passed the Stamp Act on paper, ink, and related products like wills and books four years ago. More taxes followed. These acts angered everyone here, especially the tradesmen because the taxes cut into their profits.[24] I just hope the Continentals can stop the Redcoats if it comes to a revolution."

As time passed, a divide widened between freedom supporters and most Loyalists who wanted the Crown's protection. News from New York, Boston, or Philadelphia reached Carlisle, the edge of civilization, at a turtle's pace.

MEETING JOHN HAYS

Mary spent time outdoors weeding or sweeping the porch and walkway as mild October days lingered. The wind scattered the fallen leaves. One evening near dusk, Mary was sweeping when a young man strolled by. He paused, watching her. Removing his hat, revealing coffee-brown hair tied back and clubbed, the fashion for middle-class men. Bowing slightly, he smiled at her.

"Good evening. I'm John Casper Hays, the town barber. You are Miss—"

"Mary Ludwig." She thrust her hand to shake, but he brought her fingers to his mouth. His lips grazed her knuckles. Red bloomed on her already florid cheeks. She withdrew her hand.

"Pleased to meet you." He leaned forward, his right foot extended, and bowed slightly. "Your servant, miss."

"And pleased to meet you, too." She dipped a small curtsey.

For months, the two often stopped and exchanged pleasantries. On Sunday afternoons, Hays stopped by the

---

24. Benson Bobrick, *Angel in the Whirlwind: The Triumph of the American Revolution* (New York: Penguin Books, 1997), 71.

Irvines after church during Mary's free time. They gathered pine boughs, pinecones, mistletoe, and holly at Christmas to decorate the house. Ice and snow glazed the town. At the Lutheran church Ludwig attended, choirs rehearsed Christmas hymns. Families made homemade Christmas gifts like cornhusks or rag dolls for girls, lead soldiers for boys, and whittled toys for both and squirreled them away until Christmas Eve. The house smelled of wassail and plum pudding. Beneath the holiday gaiety, a grey mood prevailed as men withdrew to the office to discuss politics.

Spring brought rain and blooming flowers. That summer, the couple spent their leisure time exploring Carlisle. Watching men haul limestone to build houses and lay cobblestones occupied an afternoon. Traveling strangers sought directions; one family needed a blacksmith to reshoe their horses. Another sought help to free a wagon mired in the mud just outside the town. Residents stopped to bid the couple a good day. They were married at the Carlisle courthouse on July 24, 1769.[25] Mary continued to work for the Irvines for the next four years until the tensions among the various factions reached Carlisle.

On January 24, 1773, Mrs. Irvine went to childbed and delivered her healthy firstborn son. His parents named him Callender, Anna's maiden name.[26]

That same year, with limestones from the quarry, builders erected the Dickinson Grammar School, which was later converted to Dickinson College. Laborers laid bricks at housing sites. Others widened trails to make roads.

25. John Landis, *A Short History of Molly Pitcher, The Heroine of the Battle of Monmouth* (Carlisle, Pa.: The Corman Print Co., 1905), 10.

26. "Dr. William Irvine," accessed at www.irvineclan.com.

3

Talk of War

Mary lived in Carlisle for eight years. At the Irvines, she fed and walked Irvine's baby when he fussed and continued her other household duties. At home, Mary fixed her husband's supper. In the evening, she mended his wool socks. "Maybe the stinking lobster-backs won't get this far west," Mary said. "If they do, we'll show them! We'll fight for our land and freedom!" She made a fist and shook it.

News and rumors raced down the Pennsylvania Turnpike from the east. Tensions mounted between the colonies and England. The king had declared the land west of the Appalachians Native tribal lands for those who fought on England's side during the French and Indian War. Britain armed the loyal tribes with muskets again to attack settlers from the west. Yet homesteaders streamed through Carlisle for free land to settle the west.

When she heard the news of King George's orders, Mary asked, "Who in the hell says people can't settle in the west? How can England force people to stay or go? Settlers will push west anyway. Here, I thought we could live our lives our way."

"Maybe it won't come to that," John said.

Enraged colonists resented the burdensome taxes and laws. They felt dues endangered their livelihood and limited their freedom. Most resented sending any of their hard-earned wages and raw materials to England. The British governors grew anxious with the rebels' rising protests.

The Continental Congress sent Benjamin Franklin to London to resolve the growing conflict. Franklin met with Lord Frederick North, governor of the colonies. When Tory governors complained about the rising rebellion, Lord North sent Franklin a stern letter that dictated England's terms for ending hostilities between the Motherland and the colonies. Franklin rejected those harsh and punishing terms that replaced colonial governors with Loyalists and closed the Boston Harbor. Colonials called the Coercive Acts Intolerable Acts. Congress then sent Franklin as an ambassador to France to seek aid.[27]

Traffic continually streamed westward. Rebels arrived at Irvine's house on appointed nights and closeted themselves in his office. Mary met Dr. Irvine's guests at the door and ushered them to his office, asking, "Tea or coffee? Wine or rum?"

The doctor sat behind his desk, waiting for the meeting. A black velvet ribbon secured his sandy hair at the nape of his neck. A matching cravat nearly hid his collar. He had a round face, kind eyes, a long, straight nose, and double chins. He wore a suit with a matching vest the color of toast.[28] He greeted the arriving men with a smile and a handshake.

27. Benson Bobrick, *Angel in the Whirlwind: The Triumph of the American Revolution* (New York: Penguin Books, 1997).

28. "Dr. William Irvine," accessed at www.irvineclan.com.

One fact Mary learned about being a servant: the men did not pay her much attention beyond a cursory nod or "Thank you" for refreshments. They spoke quietly but openly about the coming revolution. She listened and remembered the bits of conversation she overheard: "Opposing factions, Quakers refusing to take up arms. Opposed to the slave trade, Presbyterians remained neutral, and Anglicans (Loyalists/Tories) backed the Crown."[29] Other sects joined the rebellion.

The Scots-Irish who settled in Cumberland County joined the Rebellion with good reason. In 1746, English soldiers defeated the Scots Highlanders in the Jacobite Uprising at the Battle of Culloden, killing a generation of young men. So the Scots and Irish relished sailing past the blockade at night with smuggled muskets, whiskey, wine, cider, and rum. And tea.

On April 18, 1775, in Boston, Paul Revere, William Dawes, and about forty other Minutemen rode through the night warning colonists, "The Regulars (British army and navy) are coming!" Like a chain reaction, each knocked on doors, delivered the message, mounted their horses again, and rode hard to the next village. Though Redcoats caught Revere, the riders warned people in all thirteen colonies.

Clinton's flagship, the HMS *Cerebus*, led one hundred ships across the Atlantic. Ten thousand British soldiers, artillery, infantry, and mercenaries sailed into New York's harbor.[30] They forced Washington to retreat, but 10,000 Continentals penned in the British troops and took

---

29. Robert Secor, ed., *Pennsylvania 1776* (University Park, Pa.: Pennsylvania State University Press, 1975), 314.

30. Benson Bobrick, *Angel in the Whirlwind: The Triumph of the American Revolution* (New York: Penguin Books, 1997), 139.

prisoners. The battle left the British Regulars demoralized. Returning to England, humiliated by the losses, General Henry Clinton wanted to resign, but the king promoted him instead. The Crown gave him orders to take the capital, Philadelphia. When he returned, British troops had abandoned New York and occupied the capital.[31]

When Continentals met tired and hungry Redcoats at the bridge in Lexington, a standoff occurred on April 19, 1775. Stalling so locals had time to move their guns and ammunition to a safe hiding place, the colonials refused to budge. As tensions mounted, soldiers on both sides grew jittery. Both sides tried to avoid bloodshed as the Minutemen backed away. Someone fired, and then British soldiers fired into a group of Minutemen, igniting the Revolutionary War. Redeploying to Concord, the British Regulars roved from house to house, searching for armaments; finding none, they wreaked havoc on the town by burning the courthouse. This time, the citizens were forewarned about the events that occurred in Concord. Again, a skirmish ensued. Fighting guerilla style, the militia and friendly Indians fired from every direction, forcing the British to retreat.

PREPARATIONS FOR WAR

In Carlisle, families prepared for the war. News swept west about Colonial skirmishes with Redcoats and Susquehannock Indians. Citizens heard of English officers physically abusing civilians and confiscating houses for their headquarters. Soldiers rousted people from their homes, indifferent to the items they destroyed. Their soldiers stole

31. Ibid.

what they wanted—seized and killed livestock and food for their army. They blew up munitions and bridges and plundered homes. They filled wells with dirt. Crowding into alehouses, some Regulars drank too much, which loosened tongues. Many bragged about occupying Boston and New York. Cities along the Atlantic faced similar situations.

But daily life demanded time and attention not only for war plans but also for survival. After a long day at the Irvines, Mary brought leftover stew and Johnny cakes home for supper. After dinner, her husband chopped wood and stacked it in the crib he'd built. Mary sewed sleeves onto John's new shirt and hemmed handkerchiefs.

At the Irvine house, similar preparations for war were underway. Meetings included the town's leaders like Robert Callender, John Armstrong, and James Wilson. Couriers relayed news of troop movements from the cities from Washington's informants in Boston, New York, and Philadelphia. Manufacturing rifles and bullets ramped up and were stored at the Carlisle Barracks. Local men entered the void as the Proprietors' patronage disappeared with Thomas Penn's death. They felt a revolution would give them opportunities to contribute, earn money, and advance their societal position.

Most of the action thus far had focused on the port cities. Carlisle residents scurried to board up their homes, hide their valuables, and store their food in storm shelters, attics, and barns for the winter. Many tried to hide their livestock in the country, as well.

4

The Gathering Storm

Wagons loaded with supplies rolled through town. Mary darted out the door and down the street to see the commotion. An older gentleman with long grey hair was perched atop a canvas-covered wagon with several horses hitched to the back. The Conestoga wagon behind the wagon revealed only the driver. The convoy stopped, and he asked, "Excuse me, ma'am. Is there a place to eat in town?"

"An inn's down the road a good ways." Mary pointed east.

"Much obliged." He tipped his hat and slapped the horses' reins.

The third man paused by Mary and removed his hat.

"Thomas Mifflin, at your service, ma'am." He removed his tri-cornered hat and bowed slightly, using it to dust off his pants. "Former aide de camp to the General, Washington appointed me the new Quartermaster."

Mary shaded her eyes from the sun. "What's going on?"

"King George must have received The Declaration of Independence. A Continental Congress committee worked on the document, which passed and was published in Philadelphia on July 4, 1776. It's made quite a stir in the cities. It's a record of the colonists' proclaiming their rights. One sentence stands out—that we have the right to 'life, liberty, and the pursuit of happiness." Then Mifflin slapped the reins and drove east.

" Well, damn, that's quite the notion. Happiness, huh?" When John came home, Mary described the stranger. "Rebels are collecting supplies and preparing to fight. Loaded wagons and horses passed through town."

"Was it the acting quartermaster Ben Franklin?" he asked. "Word came that he was traveling north to gain support for the cause after the Boston Tea Party. In protest, rebels switched to drinking coffee."

"No, I don't think so. The soldier on horseback said he's Thomas Mifflin. General Washington just appointed him Quartermaster." Mary replied. "I never met Franklin, but I saw him onct from afar."

"Yes. Word goes that he's traveling from York. He lives in Philadelphia, is a printer and writer by trade, and is also a famous inventor. He started a library. That means people can borrow and return books for free. He invented the lightning rod and began a street-sweeping program. Oh, and he invented the rocking chair and who knows what else."

"Oh, yeah, Papa said he invented the Franklin stove," Mary remembered while she patched her husband's knee-length breeches. "Now he's into politics. One of Dr. Irvine's late-night guests said he traveled to London and France. Must be a very busy man."

"As a Patriot, he deserves more recognition than he gets," John commented.

5

Everyone Who Values Freedom

As time wore on, the couple could no longer avoid current events. In December, John told Mary, "The war has begun. I'm closing the shop and enlisting in the First Pennsylvania Artillery. Every man who values freedom will do the same." John declared. "Dr Irvine enlisted, too. Colonel Irvine will lead the first Pennsylvania line.[32]

"Of course, we must defend our homeland," Mary agreed. "England taxes stamps, paper, the tea, then what's next? Wine? The air? We should tax our exports to the Motherland and see how dem Brits like it. No wonder people smuggle liquor past the blockade."

Hays shrugged and smiled. "The sooner we can send the lobster-backs across the sea, the better."

She packed John a change of clothes and several handkerchiefs in a canvas bag. He would wear his good outfit, an overcoat, and his tricornered hat.

---

32. Brendan Morrisey, *Monmouth Courthouse 1778: The Last Great Battle of the North.* (New York: Osprey Publishing, 2004), 42–43.

"By the way, will you sew these canvas bags together after I fill them with gunpowder or 'cartridges' for the cannons?" He explained the process:

> The rammer sponges the cannon's bore to ensure no live sparks ignite the gunpowder too early, or the barrel will explode. Another covers the vent with a leather thumbstock or protector so sparks don't fly out or air isn't sucked in. The 'matrose,' or powder bearer, puts the ready-made charge bags into the cannon's bore. Then [I] flip the ramrod around to the other end and ram the cartridge into the mouth of the cannon. Another loads the cannonball. A third man lights the fuse. Then, the gunner aims and fires.[33]

The ground trembles like rolls of thunder. Then we repeat." He noticed Mary's eyes glaze over.

"Stop! EE! I didn't know it was so damn difficult. OK, let's do it." She set aside her mending to work on the cartridges.

"Uh, we have to go outside. We daren't bring gunpowder into the house. "He nodded to the flames dancing in the fireplace while mimicking an explosion. "BOOM!"

Mary jumped up, her eyes wide open.

Outside, with only a candle for light, John scooped gunpowder from a barrel into the bags, closed them, and Mary sewed tops together. Then, her husband sealed them

---

33. Colonel Thomas E. Sheperd, US Army (retired). Former Instructor at the US Army War College. Note to author, 24 March 2024.

with fish glue.[34] He stacked the cartridges in crates and ammunition boxes to be stored with the cannon. She helped him load the crates into a wagon.

He rolled his wool blanket, ax, rope, handsaw, and hunting and pocket knives into a canvas knapsack.

"Where did you get the gunpowder?" she asked.

"My lips are sealed." He smirked. "Honestly? We stole it from the British, who probably imported it. They don't guard their rear supply wagons that closely after midnight." His face bore a hint of mischief. "And the soldiers like to drink." He winked as he pulled a flask from his rucksack. He asked, "Learn any news from the big house?"

She nodded. "One, Mrs. Irvine is expecting again. She'll go to childbed in March. Two, the men are planning a strategy for battling the Redcoats. The doctor is worried because the colonists are so divided. Loyalists will fight for England. The men discussed the splintered factions as fighting runs against the Quakers' beliefs. Some native tribes will fight for the Crown, but former slaves and free Blacks should join the Continentals."[35]

Her husband nodded, listening while tossing a log into the fire.

"Looks like colonists will suffer through a long winter if the Redcoats get the upper hand," Mary sighed as she watched the flames flare.

Mrs. Irvine invited neighbor ladies to tea the next day at the mansion. They prepared bandages, knitted socks, and stitched quilts for the soldiers. Laying aside her

---

34. Richard Bell, *The Great Courses: Ordinary Americans in the Revolution* (College Park, Md.: University of Maryland, 2003).

35. Ibid.

knitting, Mary filled the teapot to heat water. Lining up cups, she dropped in tea leaves. While the tea steeped, she pulled golden scones from the pan and arranged them on a silver tray. A dollop of strawberry jam topped each one. With care, the domestic served the ladies. After dessert, the guests left, chatting as Mrs. Irvine thanked them for making supplies for the soldiers.

A TIME TO HARVEST

Like most families, the Irvines salted and smoked meat and dug the last root vegetables from their garden. Standing in the cold cellar, Mary wrapped apples in paper for winter storage. She twisted the garlic bulbs and onions with twine and hung them from the floor beams. On her next trip, Mary carried down the turnips and potatoes.

A laborer entered the house with a block of ice and carried it down to the cellar on his back with gigantic tongs. Straightening his back, he dropped the ice on the ground near the stored food. He tipped his cap and muttered, "G'day" as he left. Mary coated the block with straw so it would last longer. "Is the food safe here?" she wondered aloud. "Do we have a place to hide it?"

In the evening at the Hays's house, Mary measured and pinned a pattern of old broadsheets to cut the red cloth. She sewed the pieces together. Gently pulling the threads, Mary gathered the waist and then added a waist-band. Hays hemmed the skirt; she wore her skirts several inches shorter than fashionable women. Next, she sewed a blouse and a fitted blue jacket matching the flag's colors.

"If Colonists want freedom, we'll do our part." Mary huffed as she stitched.

Mrs. Irvine shared her news with Mary: "The British captured Dr. Irvine at Three Rivers!" on June 06, 1776.[36] Her hand flew to her chest, her head bowed while tears dripped down her cheeks. "Was he wounded? Is he in prison? If so, where? What will the Brits—or Canadians—do to him?" The letter floated to the floor.

Mary stooped over to pick up the letter, handing it to Mrs. Irvine. "He's an officer; they must treat Dr. Irvine fairly—or at least keep him alive. "Look! There's words on the back." She put the letter back in Anna's hands.

"Oh. It says William is on parole. I am not sure what that means."

Seeing Anna's face grow pale, Mary winced at her bluntness. "Who's his commanding officer?"

"General George Washington."

"O, my lands! Then Dr. Irvine will be all right."

---

36. Alan Taylor, *American Revolutions: A Continental History, 1750–1804* (New York: W.W. Norton & Co., 2016).

6

A Bold but Dangerous
Plan

The military situation was so dire that the Continental
Congress sent Ben Franklin to France again as an ambassador to seek funds, military aid, and munitions. Once
there, Franklin convinced the ambassador that France
would benefit from an American alliance. France could
hardly say no since the pamphleteer Thomas Paine had
written that France would assist the colonists. If that
country refused the request, it would lose face with other
nations. Plus, France and England had been adversaries
since the French and Indian War.[37]

By the banks of the Delaware River on Christmas Eve
1776, the Continentals and militias embarked on a bold but
dangerous mission to retreat from General Clinton's advancing army. Helped by the Marblehead regiment of fishermen,
Continental soldiers began loading 2,400 men, equipment,
and horses at sunset. The hefty, barrel-chested General Knox
barked out directions as night stole upon them. "Mind the

37. Benson Bobrick, *Angel in the Whirlwind: The Triumph of the American Revolution* (New York: Penguin Books, 1997), 348–49.

horses! Steady that cannon!" The Delaware River ran fast and frigid—ice flows bumping the flatbottom boats called scows. As they crossed the river, waves tossed the scows, sending spray across the bows. By 3:00 a.m., Washington's men landed about twelve miles north of Trenton to take out the nest of Hessians and capture their commander, Colonel Johann Rahl. Washington directed two smaller units to land south of Trenton and march north.[38]

Rain and snow pelted down, the milky mix causing poor visibility. The troops trekked roughly half the distance, forming columns for marching. As they trudged through the sludge, fog settled in. The men wearing rags around their feet had to strip the damp cloth strips off. Yet they pressed on barefooted.

A courier delivered a note warning Commander Rahl that the enemy approached. He sent his soldiers out to search the grounds, but they found no one. Thinking the incident was a false alarm, he let the men lay down their weapons and celebrate with drinks and cards. So, the Hessians celebrated Christmas.[39] They'd decorated a pine tree, perhaps the first Christmas tree in America!

When attacked before dawn, the mercenaries were surprised and hungover; thus, they were unprepared and outnumbered. They stumbled out of their tents, many in long johns. Fumbling for clothes and guns, the Hessians struggled to form a line. They succeeded at neither task. Washington's and his cousin William's regiments killed and captured a thousand enemies. Rahl was fatally wounded. The Continentals seized the enemies' weapons, artillery, and munitions and destroyed the Hessian camp.[40]

---

38. Ibid., 231–32.
39. Ibid., 232.
40. Ibid., 233.

7

Valley Forge

John Hays left for training in Valley Forge, the Continental Army's campsite near the Schuylkill River. The rural, isolated camp lay twenty-four miles north of Philadelphia. Sturdy stands of elm, oak, chestnut, and pine trees supplied the wood for the shelter the soldiers needed. He worried about his troops, roughly 11,000 soldiers ill-equipped for war, and 400 vulnerable camp followers,

Because of the threat of snow and ice, he ordered the men to build the cabins first—others he assigned to dig the latrines.

A third group constructed a circular fence for the horses.

At Valley Forge, Washington and his staff of twenty-two were headquartered in the Potts farmhouse, a sturdy, stone two-story. He joined his men at the camp daily for training. He and his generals plotted strikes against Clinton's rear brigade as the British abandoned Philadelphia. The Commander-in-Chief aimed to stop the British from retaking New York, which he'd lost the year before when Clinton first sailed into the New York

Harbor with one hundred ships loaded with men, equipment, ammunition, supplies, food, and horses.

Winter brought more snow and freezing temperatures. The frigid air stung the soldiers' ears; the wind burned their faces. Freezing temperatures brought blinding snow and dropped misery upon everyone. Washington's army and the civilians lacked the basics, like essential food, clothing, weapons, and ammunition for hunting, protection, and defense.

Pacing back and forth, General Washington considered his options.

Enlisted men, state militia members, and some officers, including Marie John Joseph, the Marquis de Lafayette, trickled in for training. Lafayette had sailed to the colonies from France. With a soft oval face and ruddy cheeks, the nineteen-year-old looked more like a dandy than a soldier, dressed in a ruffled shirt and uniform buttons running up his lapels. An idealist committed to freedom for all, he joined the troops at Valley Forge as a volunteer.

The seventeen-year-old aide de camp Alexander Hamilton watched the General's features darken. Washington's men were farmers and tradesmen, not soldiers. How could they face the world's most dominant and disciplined army and navy? Farmers used pitchforks, axes, and picks—not muskets, rifles, and cannons. As the shoes wore out, men wrapped their feet with strips of cloth. Some didn't even have shoes. Frostbite became so prevalent that the men stood on their hats. Food was dwindling. "Congress must quit stalling; we need money for everything." Frustrated, Washington bristled at his men's suffering and the stalling Congressmen.

"I can carry a missive to Mr. Hancock. Sir, we don't know how to fight like the British or Hessians, but a foreign officer has offered to help," Hamilton replied. "Remember we met him in Philadelphia? Dr. Franklin recommended him." The comely lad pivoted on his heel, marched from the Potts' farmhouse and returned with a stocky stranger wearing a spotless foreign uniform and polished knee-high boots. His translator, Pierre Duponceau, stood just behind. The General stepped outside. As tall and fit as Washington, his military bearing impressed the soldiers. The stranger saluted Washington, who remained skeptical of foreign fighters looking for fame and glory; the General nodded for the man to continue and motioned for them to walk to the edge of camp.

The officer bowed and then handed Washington Franklin's letter of introduction. He saluted. "My name is Baron Frederick Wilhelm Augustus von Steuben. I served in the Prussian military for seventeen years." He presented his military service papers. The Commander-in-Chief led von Steuben to the campsite. After touring camp for several days, he returned to Headquarters to meet with Washington.

Von Steuben said, "If I may suggest . . ." the sentence trailed off as Duponceau translated. This foreign officer politely waited for permission to share his observations, his hands clasped behind his back. Washington motioned for him to continue. 'These half-dressed raw recruits move slowly and erratically. Except for the scouts, snipers, and sharpshooters, guerilla warfare won't work against the British Army. I can train these rag-tag men to march in formation. We can speed up their drills and instill some discipline and cleanliness.

"Sir, the camp is filthy. First, your men must learn basic hygiene to stay healthy. Otherwise, we'll lose them to disease. I suggest building latrines farther from camp. Second, to take pride in their jobs, they need uniforms. Third, when they return home from fighting, some soldiers take the muskets with them—an expensive loss. Keeping records would correct that problem. Fourth, soldiers also need a universal enlistment time. Instead of one enlisting for six months and another for nine, I'd suggest a year at first. Finally, a training manual will ensure your men learn consistent fighting skills and procedures. Soldiers need to follow orders rather than argue amongst themselves." In the dark hours of that winter, von Steuben wrote *Regulations for the Order and Discipline of the United States*, Part I.[41]

The Continental, enlistees, and draftees often disagreed with state militias about territory, overlapping jobs and responsibilities. The Continental Congress approved of having a paid army. In contrast, most state militias were volunteers who guarded their states to keep the peace and punish lawbreakers for thievery, forgery, and assault. As the revolution continued, the army and militiamen learned to unite to defend all the colonies.

Washington paused and responded, "We only have a few months to stop General Clinton's army from seizing New York again; we need food, weapons, ammunition, and uniforms. I plan to block his advance in New Jersey."[42]

41. Bob Drury and Tom Calvin, *The Heart of Everything that Is Valley Forge* (New York: Simon and Schuster, 2018), 270.

42. Brendan Morrisey, *Monmouth Courthouse 1778: The Last Great Battle of the North*. (New York: Osprey Publishing, 2004), 34 (map).

"Pardon, but how do you know he'll try to take New York? Seems a full-time job occupying Philadelphia," Duponceau translated von Steuben's words.

Washington smiled. "Because that's what I would do. Besides, my informants in the major port cities track the enemies' movements for me. Clinton's men will abandon the capital and try to block the ports. All right, go ahead. See if you can whip these men into shape."

Snow piled deep on the log huts. Despite freezing temperatures, Von Steuben went to work. He taught the troops daily, using dramatic gestures. He drilled the rebels, showing them how to attach the bayonet to the musket quickly. "Aim the musket like a rifle—for the enemies' middle." He pointed to his chest. Duponceau repeated von Steuben's orders.[43] Another foreign officer from France offered to join the American cause and assured the General he was prepared to fight.

Lafayette proved as good as his word. As an officer, he drilled the men as von Steuben ordered, so Washington awarded him a brigade. Because the Frenchman lacked field experience, he commanded his brigade without pay. Eager to join the Continental Army, the young man became devoted to Washington. After the commander promoted the Frenchman, the Continental Congress put him on the payroll. More critically, Lafayette urged France to send troops, munitions, and armaments to further aid the American soldiers who lacked the basics.

Morale fell as hunger gnawed at men's stomachs because of supply chain issues: the frigid weather, the British, and Quartermaster Mifflin's ineptness. Barefooted,

---

43. Bob Drury and Tom Calvin, *The Heart of Everything that Is Valley Forge* (New York: Simon and Schuster, 2018), 252–53.

they stamped on their hats to avoid frostbite. Despite the bone-chilling cold, von Steuben's company (100 men) marched, drilled, and practiced daily. If they lagged, von Steuben swore at them in German. "*Links, rechts,* left, right! Keep moving, and you won't freeze! March double time!*"* he marched them around the campsite. Von Steuben completed an inventory, kept records, and collected muskets when men's enlistments expired. In his manual, he listed how to march, handle munitions, and operate the equipment properly. The men and locals liked this gruff stranger and followed his orders. Day by day, the men improved.[44]

Congress in 1777 finally furnished fresh supplies—guns, ammunition, and uniforms for the Continental Army. In the revolution's early years, food that the Brits stole meant colonists and the army starved. In contrast, Loyalists dined on elaborate five-course meals in the occupied eastern cities and wine, sherry, whisky, or port. At Valley Forge in 1778, oats, flour, meat, and fish kept the surviving men from starving during that harsh, frigid winter.[45] Still, the rations Washington had ordered failed to fill the recruits' bellies, but the soldiers' morale and skills improved.

---

44. Benson Bobrick, *Angel in the Whirlwind: The Triumph of the American Revolution* (New York: Penguin Books, 1997), 334–35.

45. Robert Secor, ed., *Pennsylvania 1776* (University Park, Pa.: Pennsylvania State University Press, 1975), 152–53.

8

Packing Her Bags

In Carlisle, swollen grey clouds hovered overhead. Mary left work walking to their house. Seeing her husband tramping down the street, she ran to greet him. "Oh, I'm glad to see you! You're home safe." She pushed him away playfully. "Phew, Damn it, John, you stink, I'll fill the tin tub for you. Looks like you need a decent meal, too."

"You'd be filthy too if you lived on the road. I'll not be home for long, my dear," John answered. "I've reenlisted in the Seventh Pennsylvania Regiment as a private. The army needs more men." Once inside their house, he stood his musket in the corner of the kitchen. They shared a quiet dinner and evening—the next day, the couple packed the bare necessities for his trip. The following week, John trudged east again with other enlisted men to report to Valley Forge.

In March, a courier arrived at the Irvine household.

At the back door, Mrs. Irvine cradled her newborn, Ann Nancy, who was born on March 3, 1778.[46] She called to Mary, who was boiling dirty nappies in the outside

---

46. "Dr. William Irvine," accessed at www.irvineclan.com.

cauldron. Mary tossed the last clean one over the clothes-line. The wind had calmed but still carried a bite.

"Here's a letter for you. and one for me. It looks official. Good news! General Washington won my husband's freedom, trading him for a British officer." Anna held out Mary's letter.

"That's great news! That envelope for me?" Drying her chapped hands on her apron, Mary accepted the envelope. "Um, uh, thank you." She stared at it. The rider tipped his coonskin hat and asked for water for himself and his horse. "Of course." She handed the letter to Anna. "I'll get them water," she offered. "Will you please read my letter?"

Mrs. Irvine nodded and returned to the house.

After quenching his and his mount's thirst, the rider left. Mary returned to the house to find her employer.

Mrs. Irvine said, "It's from your husband, forwarded by your parents. He wants you to join him. He misses you."

"May I go?" Mary tried to hide her excitement. "I can take supplies and food. I'll stay and keep John's unit and the doctor fed and their clothes clean."

"Go with my blessing, dear. I'll send provisions and the knitted socks with you. But come back when you're able. We need you." Irvine nodded at the baby, who was sucking her fist. Callender whizzed through the open door. "I hungry." Frigid air wafted off his coat.

"Callender, wait," Mary called after him. "Let's fix some vittles." She tucked her husband's letter into her apron pocket and hurried inside to make tea with johnnycakes and jam. Mrs. Irvine rocked, nursed the baby upstairs, and settled her in her crib. Mary tucked the toddler in for his nap.

After work, Mary packed her clothes and caps, her pewter pitcher, two tin cups, and a hatchet in a canvas knapsack. A rolled wool blanket went in next. She carried a kettle and utensils for cooking, tucked in her sewing kit, a sack with Mrs. Irvine's provisions, and flint for fires. Folding her clothes in her valise, Mary hitched a ride to Valley Forge.

9

Camp Followers

Mary Hays joined other women and children trekking
north in wagons trailing the Continental Army. A few pack
mules carried supplies and often young children. Most
tramped along on foot for hours. The wagons rumbled over
rough terrain. Exhausted mothers snapped at their hungry,
whining children. They had impossible tasks to cook, clean,
mend, bandage, and feed their families and the soldiers.
Grasping their plight, women and older children foraged for
food and dry wood. Sometimes, they found bushes loaded
with blueberries, mulberries, or crab apples. Other times,
they pilfered food from nearby farms and their enemies.

Noisy, tired, and hungry, the followers finally set up
camp at sundown. Women started fires and put the kettles
on. Welcoming scents of food over cookfires filled the
area. On some days, they had rabbit or venison for a stew.
On other days, the women coped with what they could
forage or what farmers gave them. They pilfered food
when they found some. Their hands stayed busy with the
hassle of living out of carpet bags, doing women's work,
and trying to survive.

Once there, Mary assisted other women by preparing meals, mending clothing, and building shelters for themselves. Doing laundry became a daily chore. The army provided a few tents, but not enough. Women handed out socks and quilts. They tended to the sick and chased after their children. They cleaned and bound the enlisted men's wounds using vinegar to keep infections down. Despite their best efforts, over 2,000 men died of diseases like dysentery, pertussis and smallpox.

However, April and May brought relief from the unrelenting onslaught of snow and ice. Finding shelter during spring rains presented another challenge for those without tents or covered wagons. Rain meant mud, during which wagon wheels often became mired in the sludge. Tramping through rough terrain in inclement weather wore out shoes, which added to the women's and children's stress of keeping up with the Continental Army.

"Hey, Mrs.," a fellow camper sidled alongside Mary as they trudged toward the plateau of Valley Forge surrounded by virgin timber. Until that minute, the other women had ignored Mary Hays.

"What?" she replied, treading faster. "We're almost there. See that rise? Bet a meadow's up there."

"Aren't you afeared of those officers?" The woman hitched her load higher on her back. The pots jangled. She pointed to the officers on horseback ahead leading the caravan.

"The generals? Hell, no; they're going to battle the Redcoats. They're risking their lives fighting for freedom and making a nation. 'Sides, they have more important things to do than worry about us."

"They don't take to us. Look at us like we are vermin. You can tell in their eyes and the way they avoid us."

"Well, we ain't exactly the ladies they marry or 'sociate with. Look, the first is General George Washington, Commander-in-Chief, on the white horse. He's the tallest. My husband says he's a fine man—honest, stoic and brave.

The second, I think, is Benedict Arnold. John said he's a hardened warrior but moody. He limps from a war injury up north.

The third . . .

10

The Generals at Valley Forge

On the way to their Valley Forge, sporadic skirmishes and battles broke out when the Continentals and state militias unexpectedly met enemy scouting parties. General Washington mapped out troop movements and appointed reliable officers as battalion leaders. Except for Lafayette, all officers were seasoned soldiers. Having finally arrived, the men started working.

Commander-in-Chief George Washington needs no introduction. The most seasoned officer in the Army, he grew up in Virginia; he considered himself a landowner and planter who led the Virginia militia and fought in the French and Indian War. Later, he served in the Continental Congress. His leadership qualities, martial record, and political acumen made him the most qualified for his position. After grammar school, Washington schooled himself by reading widely from the classics to military manuals. His wife, Martha, visited the camp at Christmas to offer cheer and boost morale.[47]

---

47. Stephanie Bearce, *The American Revolution: Spies, Secret Missions, and Hidden Facts* (Waco, Texas: Prufrock Press, 2015), 59.

General Benedict Arnold fought with valor during his earlier campaigns in Canada, defeating the British at Fort Ticonderoga. Wayward and hot-headed as a child, Arnold's father apprenticed him to a druggist when Benedict turned thirteen. When he finished training, he opened a shop before the war, becoming a prosperous merchant by adding stationery, quill pens, and other sundries to the drug store. During the Revolutionary War, his victories on the battlefield were sharp and decisive. In time, his allegiance would turn in part because Congress failed to promote him.[48]

Charles Lee arrived at camp. As a child, he went to military school in Switzerland. He became a soldier at age fifteen, traveling to Virginia with his father's company. Posted alone in New York, Lee seemed lost. Mohawks took him in; he married within the tribe. A career soldier, he fought in Europe and later returned to Virginia. Some Continental Congress members thought him a better leader than Washington, especially the Conway Cabal, who favored Lee. Tall and thin as a fence post, Lee's vanity, envy, and indecisiveness made him defensive and hot-tempered. He lobbied for the Commander-in-Chief's job behind Washington's back. As their letters indicate, he and Washington often argued over military matters.[49]

Nathanael Greene had a fair complexion, a comely face, a knife-sharp nose, and full lips. Born into a Quaker family, he carried those values and traits like honesty and perseverance into his job as Commander of the Southern Continental Army. Greene rode and fought with

48. Bob Drury and Tom Calvin, *The Heart of Everything that Is Valley Forge* (New York: Simon and Schuster, 2018), 76–77.

49. Brendan Morrisey, *Monmouth Courthouse 1778: The Last Great Battle of the North*. (New York: Osprey Publishing, 2004), 17–18.

Washington. He strode into camp and agreed to act as the new Continental Quartermaster, who gathered supplies for the Continental Army and its animals. However, he also wanted to keep his military post. Loyal to Washington, he executed both jobs with courage and skill.[50]

Another foreigner sat separately from the others. Young and inexperienced but eager to fight, Major General The Marquis de Lafayette met resistance at first because foreign fighters often embellished their records. He offered to serve as a volunteer without pay and acted as a liaison between his country and the colonies—a crucial role that led France to grant financial aid to America and become a significant ally.[51]

One more foreign soldier, Frederick Wilhelm von Steuben, played a pivotal role at Valley Forge. A professional Prussian soldier, he served under Frederick the Great; he set the example of *being* a soldier. He turned raw enlistees into soldiers and penned a training manual called "The Blue Book," which the army used until 1812. He commanded his brigade,[52] drilling his men daily despite the bone-chilling cold and the soldiers' meager accommodations.

As a child, Henry Knox, a Boston bookseller, showed a propensity for math. He read widely, studying engineering to learn how to move unwieldy objects. A beefy, barrel-chested man with a boyish face, the man topped 300 pounds. At one point, he volunteered to retrieve the cannons, weapons, and ammunition when the British abandoned Ft. Ticonderoga after their defeat. Knox also

---

50. "Nathanael Greene," *Georgia Encyclopedia*, accessed at: https://www.georgiaencyclopedia.org/articles/history-archaeology/nathanael-greene-1742-1786/.

51. Bob Drury and Tom Calvin, *The Heart of Everything that Is Valley Forge* (New York: Simon and Schuster, 2018), 29–31.

52. Ibid., 252–53.

spearheaded crossing the Delaware on Christmas Eve by bellowing orders to move men, boats, and horses above the sounds of the river. He commanded the Continental artillery.[53]

The assembly included "Mad" Anthony Wayne. His intense eyes, woolly black eyebrows, and frizzy white hair gave him an air of authority. Trusted and tested by battle, Anthony was a flexible leader but critical of his superior officer's (Lee's) approach to fighting.[54] Wayne trusted Washington's practical and methodical strategies; the commander-in-chief could see the big picture.

Daniel Morgan's elite riflemen were scouting but would join the march to Trenton. In likeness, he resembled the Commander-in-Chief. He culled the best shooters from different militia and the army's companies; they dressed in fringed buckskin shirts, long pants, and bi-cornered hats. Their movements covered hot spots like the Battle of Monmouth, surprise raids, and—with advance notice, operated as snipers. His unit also used similar tactics like guerilla warfare and weapons like tomahawk throwing they acquired from Native tribes.[55]

WAR COUNCIL

The generals at Valley Forge debated the best approach to New Jersey. "Henry Clinton commands the British army with brothers Generals William and Admiral Richard Howe and John Burgoyne. Cornwallis has several brigades—the artillery, infantry, and cavalry. The Queen's

---

53. Brendan Morrisey, *Monmouth Courthouse 1778: The Last Great Battle of the North.* (New York: Osprey Publishing, 2004), 76–77.

54. Ibid., 44.

55. Albert Zambone, "Daniel Morgan: A Revolutionary Life" episode on *American History*, C-SPAN3, viewed May 6, 2019.

Rangers, an elite unit of fighters, are also with them. Who knows how many thousands of Hessians they've hired."

Washington spread a large map across the table. "I see two approaches to New Jersey." He traced his finger east. "Clinton will abandon Philadelphia and travel south and cross the Delaware River to Crosswicks. That's the straightest route. He might proceed to Sandy Hook, then sail on a boat straight into the New York harbor. My men will go north to Doylestown, east to Rocky Hill, and then south to Trenton. We'll cut Clinton off in New Jersey."[56]

"Sir, begging your pardon, but that's a long way around. Our infantry will be exhausted. We should use a two-pronged attack," General Greene suggested. He pointed to a more direct route across the middle of the map.

"Or three-pronged," said Lafayette, his finger tracing the third direction. "The good news—the British Regulars do not know the terrain. That will slow them down. That's one advantage we have."

"Yeah," Von Steuben agreed. "*Das ist gut.*"

"Trenton is our goal. Why?" asked Arnold.

"Because my informants say that the Hessian garrison is a weak link with a skeleton crew. Besides, the garrison is blocking our way; our goal is to stop Clinton." Washington explained and then continued.

"Arnold, you're the new governor of Philadelphia. Take your men and assess the situation. See how much damage the Redcoats did to the city. Inventory what's left and list what we need. Send me coded messages by courier."[57]

---

56. Brendan Morrisey, *Monmouth Courthouse 1778: The Last Great Battle of the North.* (New York: Osprey Publishing, 2004), 34 (map).

57. Ibid., 29.

The Commander-in-Chief showed each general the routes across Pennsylvania and New Jersey to fight the British near Monmouth Courthouse by the end of June. "Engage and attack Clinton's retreating men. Harass their flanks. Take or destroy their supply wagons.

"My brigades will take the northern route. Lee and Marshall will take the southern route. Lafayette and Morgan's men will ride with me, but you'll be under Lee's command during the battle. We'll split the troops at Hopewell, a direct route to Trenton."[58]

Off they marched, making good time. Hundreds of miles lay before them while the civilian wagon train trailed behind. Thundershowers pelted soldiers and the travelers; drenched clothes plastered their skin. Slogging through the mud slowed the columns, especially when wagon wheels became mired in the sludge. Trudging along rough terrain, women with small children strived to keep up. At times, mounted soldiers drifted back to offer children rides. Comfort women, or prostitutes, brought up the rear, keeping to themselves until sundown. When discovered, the Continentals drove the ladies of the night out of camp.[59]

At Doylestown on June 23, Washington dispatched Generals Lafayette and Daniel Morgan south to Trenton. He led his battalion east. Mary followed the southern route to visit her mother before the battle and rejoined the march. She kept to Indian trails with senses alert to tramping horses and hazards like rattlesnakes and wild animals. If she saw pockets of Redcoats, she hid. She recognized the Mohawks, Continental allies, because of their strip of standing hair. As for the Susquehannock tribes

58. Ibid., 40.
59. Ibid., 37–38.

who fought for England, she ran for cover in the woods or behind boulders. She made a nest of pine needles and leaves at night and wrapped herself in her blanket. When she could, she hitched a ride to Trenton.

11

The Battle at Monmouth Courthouse

Arriving at Monmouth Courthouse on the eve of June 27, Mary found a place among the Continental wagons to camp. Rows of corn stalks rustled warnings. Trudging north, she saw faces she recognized. "Good evening." She greeted several other wives who were sweaty, tired, and dirty from the long march. A few nodded but kept to their tasks. Young children clung to their mother's skirts. She heard older children rustling in the trees. "Tomorrow's the big day," one weary woman said.

"Yep. You're damned straight." Hays nodded toward the tree line. "The battlefield is just on the other side of the trees." Her warning worked; some women picked up their skirts edged in dirt and dried mud to chase after their progeny. As dusk dropped, Mary found a spring of fresh water. She gathered twigs from the woods to light a fire. Once the kindling caught, she teepeed dry sticks and laid dry, dead logs on top. Sharpening two stout, "Y" shaped sticks, Mary hammered them into the ground on either side of the fire. Then, laid a wet, green branch across the sticks. As the fire flared, she put on the tea kettle. Mary opened the butcher paper her mother had given her as the water heated. Pouring hot water into her cup, she dropped tea leaves in to steep and set aside the tea. She hooked her cooking pot over the fire. Anna Irvine had packed flour, coffee, jerky, bread, cheese, dried carrots, and apples.

Into the pot went water, dried beef, and vegetables. While that simmered, Mary took her hatchet to the woods to chop thick branches for a lean-to. Mary thatched a roof of pine branches. And then stuffed the chinks with moss to catch the dampness. Underneath, she put her rolled blanket and a canvas pack. When John and his friend John McCauley found her, they quietly ate and drank tea. Her husband's mate left after dinner. Mary flayed one end of a small pine stem and brushed her teeth. She slept in her chemise.

"Wish me luck tomorrow," Hays whispered in her ear. They spent the night together. Hays dressed and left before daybreak.

THE MONMOUTH COURTHOUSE BATTLE

At dawn's first light, Mary cobbled her things together. Already sweaty, she pulled on a slip, petticoats, an under-skirt, and her new gathered skirt. Over her homespun blouse, the woman donned her fitted jacket. Tucking her waves under a ruffled cap, she slung the bag of bandages on her back and grabbed her pitcher. Bunching the material in her hand, she hiked up her skirts and trudged northeast, following John's directions.

Enlisted men had mounted palisades—logs roughly eight feet, six inches in diameter, sharpened at both ends and thrust into the ground, angled in front of all the cannons. Others constructed earthworks by digging trenches and piling up little dirt hills for the enemies to stumble in or over.

Acres of vast farmland and meadows encircled the Monmouth Courthouse. Across the street from the courthouse, St. Peter's church faced the road. From north to south, acres and acres of forests opened upon a grassy central meadow; other grasslands radiated out from the central one, forming a starfish. The Colonial Army held the ground near Spotswood North down to Middle Brook. The four Pennsylvania brigades (100 men each), including Brigadier General Irvine's Seventh, spanned the distance between the trees. John Hays served as a gunner and then a rammer in this regiment. Several Virginia and Maryland state militias joined Pennsylvania's brigades. They blocked the route north between the Parsonage and Craig's farms. To the east, six Continental brigades flanked the tree line.[60]

Carrying a ramrod, John Hays crossed a meadow to a slight ridge topped with a stacked stone fence overrun with creepers. The stones had crumbled in places, notching 'Vs.' in the wall. Infantry soldiers stepped through the gaps. A line of six cannons stood guard south of the Perrine Farm and the Ridge. Twelve more cannons faced the British infantry near the Ker farm. General Lee's men were to approach from the south of the courthouse—but no sign of his brigades in sight.

---

60. Melissa Lukeman Bohrer, *Glory, Passion, and Principle: The Story of Eight Remarkable Women at the Core of the Revolution* (New York: Atria Books, 2003).

Over the rise, Continentals marched across a furrowed field. Four men clustered around one howitzer. The rest of Wayne's men and Maxwell's infantry had positioned themselves in the Cider Orchard. Just south in the Continentals' direct line of fire, Sir John Grey's entire divisions of foot guards formed battle lines.

Across the meadow, two divisions of British Dragoons (one mounted, one on foot) with a row of ten cannons south of the Ker farm faced Layfette's and part of Wayne's division. The Queen's Rangers took position behind the cannons. A second line of British Hessians and foot soldiers guarded St. Peter's Church. Others blocked the road to Middleton. Word reached Washington that Lord Cornwallis had left for Middleton, but Sir Clinton's rearguard was returning.

Behind them, mosquitoes buzzed and bit. Irksome gnats flew into the soldiers' faces as the temperature climbed higher and higher. Visible heat shimmered before them. For want of water, the tree leaves wilted. The high grasses drooped. Soldiers grew thirsty, anxious, and impatient.

Drumsticks clicked against the rim, setting feet marching. A second boy played a fife. The sweet notes carried across the meadow. A third held a blue flag with a circle of thirteen stars. As the day star inched higher, it bleached the eastern sky and heated the air to 100 degrees. Temperatures, tension, and tempers climbed. Wading between corn rows, Mary Hays found her husband.

As she approached, John patted the cannon on the end. "This is mine. I use the sponge end to swab the cannon with water." A second soldier put his thumb over the vent to avoid air being sucked into the cannon. Then I flip the rod to ram the cartridge in." He shoved the gunpowder cartridge into the cannon; another soldier loaded the cannonball. John pulled Mary to the ground. "Cover your head! Plug your ears!" A third man lights the fuse. Then the gunner fires. The cannon cracked and recoiled; the shot exploded from the barrel and bowled over several charging foot soldiers carrying fixed bayonets. A Continental soldier retrieved the fallen Redcoats' muskets from their broken, bleeding bodies. All down the line, the action repeated.

"Holy shit! That's loud." Shaking as the adrenalin kicked in, Mary pushed herself up and dusted off her skirts. Flocks of birds scattered from the trees in panic; a lone hawk glided high above the trees, hunting. A strange silence followed.

Her husband said, "See that next rise?" He pointed north. "Fresh water's in the little valley—a spring."

"Yes, I found it last night."

They heard British troops advancing. General Wayne's and LaFayette's men fired, pushing into the cream of the British infantry, backed by ten howitzers. The British volleys beat Generals Wayne's and Lafayette's men behind the treeline.[61]

Mary spotted several wooden buckets stacked against the tree trunks that formed a ragged line behind the stone fence. *Buckets are for the cannon, and a pitcher and dipper are for drinking water.* Her skirts and petticoats hampered her movements. She heard, "Molly, bring water." The sun streamed down on them; sweat trickled down her face.

---

61. Brendan Morrisey, *Monmouth Courthouse 1778: The Last Great Battle of the North.* (New York: Osprey Publishing, 2004), 42–43 (map).

Her clothes were plastered to her skin. "Molly, water the cannons." Striping off her jacket, Mary grabbed a pitcher and bucket and darted back to the stream. Plunging the containers into the stream, she filled them and lugged them back. Thirsty soldiers begged for a dipper of water. Back and forth, she raced, bringing water to the Continentals and pouring buckets over the cannons. Trip after trip took hour after hour. Between cannon blasts, the rammer swabbed the cannon inside and out after each volley. Otherwise, a stray spark could ignite the big guns too early and explode them.

Suddenly, John Hays dropped to the ground. *The enemy returned fire.* Mary stooped beside the cannon to check—he was breathing! Looking at his dark hair, his face perspiring, she noted pain in his eyes. "Are you bleeding? He shook his head. First, she ran her eyes and hands over his body and gave her husband a few sips of water. "How about you guys carry him to the shade?" she asked his team. She rolled up her jacket. "Put this under his head."

A sergeant stepped into view. He wore a doublet, hose, federalist blue knee-length breeches, and a sweat-drenched shirt. "Pull this cannon back offline."[62]

Mary jumped up and said, "I'll man his cannon." Beads of sweat dripped down her face and dampened her armpits.

Looking down at her dirty, scratched bare feet, he frowned, then nodded. "Go ahead. You can try. We'll need water soon. Wait until the Brits get closer, then shoot." He wiped the sweat from his face.

---

62. Ibid.

Because British officers wore wigs, heavy plumed hats, and wool uniforms, fifty-four soldiers toppled over from dehydration that day, the tongues lolling out and unseeing eyes staring at the sky.

Von Steuben led his men behind the stone fence about fifty yards away. He motioned the flank to move left. Sheltered by a line of trees, the militia, Scots in kilts and berets, and Continentals assembled, muskets ready. They planned to surround and rout the British.[63]

The British infantry advanced in formation, boots stamping a refrain. Time stalled. Again, Mary grabbed the bucket handle, hiked to the next ridge, and padded down the slope—her bare feet kicking pebbles into rippling water as they smacked the stream. No time to enjoy the stunning scenery, Mary sank the bucket, capturing clear, cold water. She splashed her face and hair and gulped handfuls of water. Wetting two handkerchiefs, she tied them around her neck; back at the line of cannons, she pulled off one and laid it on John's forehead.

Back at her cannon, she swabbed the barrel. Rammed the gunpowder cartridge in and stood aside, her feet planted wide to steady herself. From the enemy's side, a cannon ball flew between her legs, searing away half of her skirt and petticoat. Private Joseph Martin later wrote about the incident in his journal, published after the war.

"Good thing that ball didn't aim higher," she quipped. The men laughed. The sergeant who let her man her husband's cannon yelled, "Nice work, Sergeant Molly." She proudly used that title for the rest of her life.

---

63. Bob Drury and Tom Calvin, *The Heart of Everything that Is Valley Forge* (New York: Simon and Schuster, 2018), 176.

Noise and harsh heat climbed into the clearing. Metal clashing, saddles creaking, and shouting commands riled the meadow. A rifle cracked the air; arrows shot from trees—the screams of the dying. The smoke stung the eyes and concealed the battlefield. Wounded officers fell from their horses.

Molly gasped for air as the battle raged. Other women carried water to parched soldiers but didn't join the battle that day. Repeatedly, Mary grabbed the bucket and pitcher and trudged toward the stream. She sank them into the water, climbed the ridge, and toted water to the soldiers. She extended the ladle, her arm and shoulder muscles aching. Cannons recoiled. As smoke and gunfire choked the air, the Redcoats charged again. Ragged lines of Continentals and militia drove the Redcoats back. Three of Lafayette's regiments advanced, but the British infantry, cavalry, and Hessian Grenadiers beat them back.[64]

From the south came shouting and cannon blasts amid chaotic fighting. Like a red river, lines of redcoats with white bands crisscrossing their chests marched in formation, bayonets protruding from the muskets. The sun winked off the lethal blades, blinding the rebels.

---

64. Brendan Morrisey, *Monmouth Courthouse 1778: The Last Great Battle of the North.* (New York: Osprey Publishing, 2004), 42–43 (map).

A 1907 portrait of Washington and Lafayette at Valley Forge by John Ward Dunsmore

Washington and wife visiting the troops (courtesy of the Smithsonian)

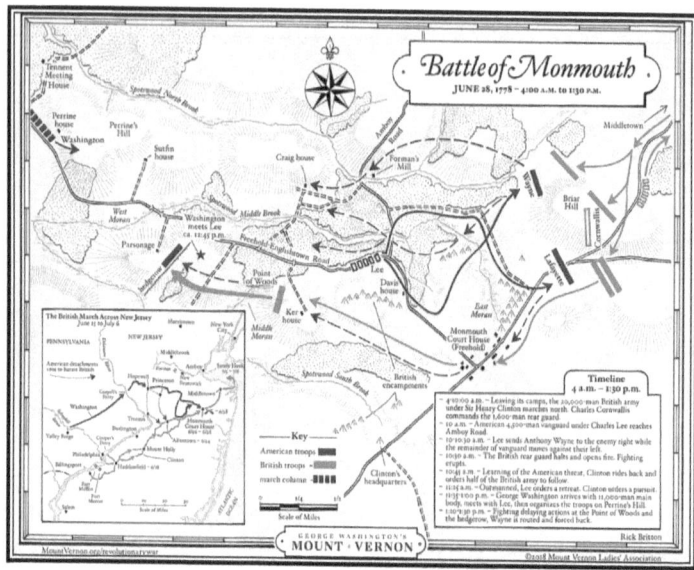

Battle of Monmouth map (courtesy of Mount Vernon)

Battle of Monmouth on 28th June 1778 in the American Revolutionary War

Washington confronting General Lee at the Battle of Monmouth

Old Monmouth Courthouse

Molly Pitcher at the Battle of Monmouth on 28th June 1778 in the American Revolutionary War: picture by Franz Ludwig Catel

Molly Pitcher depicted by Currier and Ives

Molly Pitcher grave in Carlisle

12

Lee's Retreat

As he and his men approached the battle site, a scout told General Lee the British General Cornwallis had already left Monmouth Courthouse, marching his brigades east toward Middletown. Lee then ran into General Maxwell, who seemed confused about the attack plan, but Lee issued his subordinate no orders. Lee advanced on his mount, leading his men forward. But General Clinton's rearguard surprised them. Clinton had put his best-mounted rangers and infantry Dragoons at the rear. A volley of British muskets and cannon balls mowed the rebels down. Lee ordered a retreat despite Washington's orders to advance. The ragged line broke; without orders from their commander, the soldiers fled for the tree line.

A blur on a white horse, Washington galloped across the clearing, swearing, shouting at the men. "Form a line. Advance! Damn it to Hell, Lee, you're a general! Act like one! Get your men to charge. Fight!" Washington held his ground, the barrage of musket fire erupting around him. His favorite mount, Nelson, seemed unfazed by the musket volleys. Lunging across the saddle, gesturing madly, Washington shouted at the retreating flanks. Furious and fierce, the general raced back, shouting, "Lee, I'm relieving you of your command!"[65] Lee left the battlefield, humiliated.

To Lee's men, he yelled, "Follow me! Reform the line." Slowly, the line filled and straightened as Redcoats advanced. On cue, Von Steuben's forces joined Washington's. The Highlanders followed suit. General Daniel Morgan's elite rifle unit thundered into the fray, firing at Redcoat officers. Von Steuben took over Lee's command and continued battling the never-ending line of British and Hessians.

The cannon thundered and coughed smoke; the ground shook; the heat shimmered in serpentine waves. More Redcoats drew closer, bayonets fixed. The Continentals' and militia's left and right flanks took positions to surround the enemy. 'Sergeant,' Mary sponged the rod and rammed it into the cannon all afternoon.

At nightfall, dead rebels and Redcoats littered the field, reeking like rotten meat. Women scudded out of the woods to steal the fallen soldiers' clothes, boots, and weapons. The Commander-in-Chief ordered his men off the battlefield. "We'll bury our dead and then rest the night. We attack again at daybreak, so sleep on the ground and get in formation at the cock's crow."[66]

By dawn's early light, the Continentals marched across the ruined meadow. Clinton had escaped across the Delaware River, much like Washington had crossed it to surprise the mercenaries on Christmas Day, 1776. Officers, enlisted men, the state militias, and Highlanders

---

65. Ibid.
66. Ibid., 61–62.

pounded one another on their backs, shouted, and celebrated. "The Regulars retreated! We beat them!" But the cost numbered 362 Continental and militia soldiers dead; England reported 364 men killed, with over 200 British and Hessians deserted or missing, and Washington's men captured over 40 British Regulars.[67] Other sources claim far more soldiers lost their lives on both sides.

The Battle of Monmouth, the hottest day of action during the Revolutionary War, ceased. If not a win, the rebels fought the Imperial British army, infantry, cavalry, and mercenaries to a draw. Men whose enlistment ended returned their muskets to Von Steuben and went home.

On July 4, General Washington had General Lee court-marshaled for insubordination and misconduct, showing little respect for his Commander-in-Chief. Dr. Irvine served on the panel that stripped Lee of his military rank and benefits. Washington promoted Dr. Irvine to Colonel and assigned him the command of Fort Pitt until the war's end. The doctor purchased land there.

Helping her husband hobble back to camp, the couple packed up and headed toward Trenton to visit Mary's mother and share the good news. She was with child.[68]

Though too weak to talk and walk, John smiled and nodded.

---

67. Ibid., 76.
68. Ibid., 77.

13

Homeward Bound

Returning to Carlisle, the couple took turns carrying little John strapped to their chests or backs. They bought a place on South Street, and Mary returned to work at the Irvines, taking wee John with her.

The first four Irvine children were born in Carlisle. Callender had turned seven, and Ann Nancy, two. In 1780, Anna Irvine delivered her third child, Mary, who lived one year. In 1782, Anna had a son, William, on November 11. After moving to Fort Pitt, the household grew when Elizabeth arrived four years later. Washington assigned Irvine to command Fort Pitt, where the family relocated. Mary Bullen was born in 1788, Armstrong in 1792, Rebecca in 1794, twins James and John in 1796, and Martha in 1799. When grown, Callender farmed the land, and Will added a dry goods store, farmer's market, etc., turning the family business into an enterprise.[69]

After Mary's first husband died, she married John McCauley, who'd fought with them at Monmouth

69. Kerri Alexander, "Mary Ludwig Hays (1754-1832)" at National Women's History Museum viewed at: https://www.womenshistory.org/education-resources/biographies/mary-ludwig-hays.

Courthouse. Word spread that the second marriage failed. In Carlisle, he worked as a day laborer. After running through Mary's inheritance, the man died or disappeared. People gossiped, "He liked his drink."

To support herself and her son, Mary worked for Carlisle, cleaning the courthouse for fifteen dollars and other public buildings for about twenty dollars a week. She also worked for Dr. Foulke. For a time, Mary lived in a stone building on the grounds of the former Carlisle Indian Industrial School; Mary cooked, watched children, and mended uniforms for the soldiers at the Barracks.[70] During her last decade, she moved in with her son John and his family.

Years later, Sergeant Molly walked several miles to meet General Washington and a contingent of army's soldiers who stopped in Carlisle on the way to quash the Whisky Rebellion in 1794.[71]

In 1822, the Pennsylvania legislature granted Mary Ludwig Hays McCauley, Carlisle's Molly Pitcher, a forty-dollar annual pension. The Pennsylvania House revised the bill from "widow of a soldier" to "services rendered" during the war. Several witnesses, including a camp doctor, verified Sergeant Molly's identity and battlefield valor. They included her son John and her grandson John Hays, who related his grandparents' stories. A neighbor, Mrs. Barbara Park, and Dr. Foulke's wife, Harriet, said that Mary, in later years, was "florid, stout, talkative, and coarse but kind." Another said, "She swore like a sailor.[72]

---

70. "Dr. William Irvine," accessed at www.irvineclan.com.

71. John Landis, *A Short History of Molly Pitcher, The Heroine of the Battle of Monmouth* (Carlisle, Pa.: The Corman Print Co., 1905), 28.

72. Melissa Lukeman Bohrer, *Glory, Passion, and Principle: The Story of Eight Remarkable Women at the Core of the Revolution* (New York: Atria Books, 2003), 161.

Dr. William Irvine, Mary's former employer, who fought at the Monmouth Courthouse, also knew her.

Mary Ludwig Hays McCauley spent her last decade living with her son and grandson. John's family lived in the limestone two-story on Bedford and North Streets. Historians believe Mary lived in the smaller log cabin next to the main house. She died in 1832 and was buried in Carlisle's Old Graveyard.[73]

---

73. John Landis, *A Short History of Molly Pitcher, The Heroine of the Battle of Monmouth* (Carlisle, Pa.: The Corman Print Co., 1905), 20.

14

The Legend

Forty-four years later, Carlisle erected a suitable tombstone over her grave. The Patriot Sons of America collected $5,000 for a 24-pound howitzer from Gettysburg for her gravesite. In 1905, Carlisle topped the monument with a bronze statue. An American flag unfurled as Nellie Kramer, Hays-McCauley's great-granddaughter, raised it. Five thousand people—the most to attend any memorial in Carlisle—cheered.[74]

The legendary exploits depict one woman's bravery under fire. One writer stated that "Molly Pitcher" represents the mother who nurtures and protects. Another source claims no single "Molly Pitcher" exists. However, the facts—separated from the myths—indicate the woman from Carlisle is 'most likely' the Molly Pitcher who fought at Monmouth. She contributed by sponging the cannon and carrying water to the soldiers under fire. She and other women bound the men's wounds. They scrubbed clothes clean on washer boards and cooked and mended clothes. For her bravery and patriotic duty at The

---

74. Ibid., 40.

Battle of Monmouth, Carlisle's Molly Pitcher became one of the Revolutionary War's heroines.

Continentals, militiamen, and women fought for the ground they lived on and for their "inalienable rights: life, liberty, and the pursuit of happiness." Jefferson's words in the Declaration of Independence were a radical concept then. Europeans doubted the colonists would succeed. France's money, supplies, and men aided the Continentals, but the British and Hessians had the advantage of commanding an experienced, well-trained army, navy, and cavalry. Thomas Paine's *Common Sense* and other pamphlets stirred the rebels' ire, changed people's minds, and gave credence to a union. In "The American Crisis," he penned a persuasive essay:

> These are the times that try men's souls; the summer soldier and the sunshine patriot will, in this crisis, shrink from the service of his country, but he that stands it now deserves the love and thanks of man and woman. Tyranny, like hell, is not easily conquered, yet we have this consolation with us, that the harder the conflict, the more glorious the triumph.[75]

Washington—a man who led the rebellion and revolution, guided deeply divided colonists toward union. A superb military strategist and daring leader, the 6'2" general struck an imposing figure. Though the Colonials could not count The Battle of Monmouth as a win, they forced the British to retreat. Clinton retreated, sending

75. Thomas Paine, "The Crisis," viewed at https://www.ushistory.org/paine/crisis/c-01.htm.

troops and supplies up the Delaware but keeping 9,000 men with him on the march to New York.[76]

Thousands of men, women, and children (fifes, drummers, and flag bearers) across thirteen colonies gave their efforts, careers, and lives to the cause of freedom. History has divulged the courageous actions of Americans, French, Indians, and Blacks who led the colonials to victory when Cornwallis surrendered to Washington at Yorktown. The triumph caused quite a sensation by uniting a divided nation and beating the world's most significant and best army and naval fleet during the 1700s.

One small yet essential and much-disputed story of Mary Ludwig Hays McCauley's actions attests to the determination, bravery, and perseverance that helped turn the tide at Monmouth Courthouse and thus the war and forged a path to victory. Her statue rises above the others in Carlisle's Old Graveyard and reminds all of her heroism. By stepping forward and manning her husband's cannon and carrying water to thirsty soldiers while dodging enemy gunfire, Mary Ludwig Hays, Carlisle's "Molly Pitcher," contributed to America's independence.

76. Benson Bobrick, *Angel in the Whirlwind: The Triumph of the American Revolution* (New York: Penguin Books, 1997), 343.

Timeline of Mary Ludwig Hays McCauley

1754 Born October 13, died January 22. 1832 (78 yrs old), buried in Carlisle's Old Graveyard

1763 After Pontiac's Rebellion (Native American uprising), Lord North issued George III's edit: No white settlement beyond the Appalachians angered settlers.

1765 British Parliament levied a Stamp tax upon the American colonies on most paper products. Patrick Henry's response, "Taxation w/o representation is tyranny," in the Virginia statehouse became the American rebels' mantra

1768 Mary Ludwig moves to Carlisle

1769 MLH Served as domestic for Dr. and Anna Irvine, Carlisle physician & wife, who settled in Carlisle 1763; first four Irvine children born in Carlisle, eldest born in January. Marries John Casper Hays, a barber in Carlisle, on July 24, at age 16

1773 Boston Tea Party December 16. Boston, Massachusetts, protest of taxes: The Sons of Liberty, disguised as Indians, tossed over 100 crates of tea into the harbor.

1775   Hay's husband John enlisted in the 1st Pennsylvania Artillery as a gunner for one year. April 19: Battles of Lexington and Concord

1776   Dr. Irvine enlisted as Colonel in the 7th Pennsylvania Line, was captured at Three Rivers Battle, "on parole," and later traded for a British officer. The Continental Congress passed The Declaration of Independence on July 4th, thirteen American Colonies independent from England. Brits retaliated with harsh punishments for colonists. Margaret Corbin was permanently disabled in the Battle at Fort Washington; her husband was killed.

1777   J. C. Hays reenlists in the 6th Pennsylvania Regiment, Private. Gen. G. Washington winters with troops at Valley Forge to head off Clinton's army, retaking New York; von Steuben teaches Continentals to fight like "line" British rather than guerilla warfare, march in formation, drill with muskets, etc. Courier sent a w/letter from John, asking his wife to join him at Valley Forge.

1778   Washington brokers trade for Dr. Irvine, appointed as commander of the 7th Pennsylvania Regiment. Battle of Monmouth on June 28, the hottest day of action, over 100 degrees. MLH carries water back and forth for men and to cool down cannons from the 'well,' or spring. John, injured or dehydrated, fell, and his cannon was ordered to the rear (to avoid capture). MLH steps in and mans the cannon, firing round after round.

(soldiers call her Sgt.). Gen. Lee orders men to retreat; Washington takes command and pulls the line together. In the night, Clinton's army retreats across the Delaware. Before returning to Carlisle, Ludwig-Hays has a son, John.

1779   Margaret Corbin receives $50 annual pension from Pennsylvania for bravery in war; manned husband's cannon until seriously injured—arm. "Dirty Kate." The first woman to receive a lifelong pension from military service.

1794   MLH sees Washington/troops rendezvous in Carlisle to put down the Whisky Rebellion

1800   Corbin died on January 16. John Hays died (Various dates because facts are uncertain); MLH remarries George McKolly (McCauley): various spellings, comrade.

1822   Pennsylvania Legislature grants MLH annual pension $40, payable $20 twice a year on February 14. Bill 265 was revised to read "for services rendered" rather than "widow of a soldier." Gov. Joseph Heister (No record of federal pension in her name(s). MLH lived in a stone guard house at Carlisle Indus Ind. The school (Carlisle Barracks), cooking and cleaning; also worked for Dr. Foulk; MHM moved into her son's stone home w/connecting log house at the corner of North and Bedford St. (where the church now stands), lived with w/grandson until her death. Witnesses who substantiated MLH's history: grandson, Mrs. Barbara Park, Harriet Foulk. Mary lived in the borough for 40 years. Described later as "stout, florid, coarse but kind, helpful' (Landis 16)

1832   Hays McCauley dies, buried in Old Carlisle cemetery.

1876   Stone marking her grave

1892   James Martin exhumed the body on May 3 over confusion about who was buried there. Female remains were buried beneath children's coffins.

1904   Patriot Sons of America Committee to commission a cannon—24 lb. howitzer, carriage made in Gettysburg, raised $5,000.

1905   Over 127 years after the Battle of Monmouth, the unveiling of the monument of Revolutionary War heroine with a parade, 5,000 attended the event— Most for any memorial in Carlisle. Great-great granddaughter Nellie Kramer raised the flag.

Afterword

The Monmouth Courthouse battle was more complex than I depicted; Thousands of participants contributed to the War of Independence. Because I focus narrowly on Mary Ludwig Hays McCauley, I recount the events that led up to that particular battle. For example, Senior Military Officer Henry Knox (later the Secretary of War) led several battalions and organized Crossing the Delaware—his booming voice relating Washington's orders. Daniel Morgan's Rifle Brigade led the army's best sharpshooters culled from all Continental regiments. They carried the new Kentucky or Pennsylvania long rifle—more accurate weapons than muskets or Blunderbusses.

I omitted many exciting facts about the participants:

Aaron Burr's horse was shot out from under him during the battle; he later shot and killed Alexander Hamilton in a duel because Hamilton voted for Thomas Jefferson for President. The contretemps among officers, especially between Generals Washington and Charles Lee, surprised me.

New Jersey, Maryland, and Virginia also sent troops to Monmouth Courthouse. Patrick Henry's famous words, "Give me liberty or give me death," showed how keenly he valued freedom. The Brits captured, tried, and hanged Nathan Hale for being an American spy who said, "I only regret that I have but one life to give to my country." Benedict Arnold turned bitter and betrayed his country because he felt slighted when Congress failed to promote him. He married a Loyalist, Peggy Shippen, who befriended and entertained the British spy, Major Andre. Arnold planned to hand over West Point to the British but failed. He escaped execution by following his wife to England. Major Andre was condemned and executed by hanging.

While the British abandoned Philadelphia, Andre trashed Benjamin Franklin's house, destroying antique furniture and memorabilia, some of which the inventor brought from France and England. This destruction seemed typical of the Brits, revealing their disdain for colonials.

During the Monmouth Courthouse battle, "Mad" Anthony Wayne's and Lafayette's divisions were separated when the Brits initially charged, driven back to the Ker farm, where they regrouped in the woods and charged.

Regarding the Monmouth Courthouse battle, official numbers from different sources vary, but they claim over 300 Continentals and 364 British soldiers died, fifty-four from dehydration. Twenty-six Hessian officers died, 400 wounded, and twenty-two deserted. Americans also captured forty prisoners.[77] Despite the opposition, critics, and an uncertain Congress, the rebels endured the hardships, resisted, and persevered.

Once trained, Von Steuben noted that the Americans, once trained, would be "formidable foe" and fierce military power; America owes him a debt of gratitude. Uniting the colonies, facilitating military training and maneuvers, and valiant fighting of thousands, the Continentals succeeded. Hundreds of camp followers, including Mary Ludwig Hays McCauley, Carlisle's "Molly Pitcher," helped America become independent. For that reason, Carlisle claims and celebrates her contributions.

---

77. Brendan Morrisey, *Monmouth Courthouse 1778: The Last Great Battle of the North*. (New York: Osprey Publishing, 2004), 76.

Glossary

Armoire – Large wood cabinets for storing clothing.

Artillery – heavy guns that use solid balls, mounting on wagons

Bayonet – long doubled-edged knife mounted on a musket

Breastworks – field fortifications thrown up for defense

Brigade – a military unit containing at least two regiments (100 soldiers)

Broadsheet – news printed on both sides of a sheet of paper

Cartridges – bags packed with gunpowder used to shoot cannons.

Calico – inexpensive cotton material used to make dresses

Chamber pots – round portable porcelain containers used to hold urine, kept in bedrooms for overnight use

Clubbed – Men's long hair tied at the nape of the neck with a ribbon and turned under.

Comfort women – prostitutes

Continentals – the rebel soldiers enlisted by Congress and state militias

Corn crib – a wood container with slats for corn cobs to dry, used to wipe

Credence – lends credit to a belief

Dandy – a flamboyant male who dressed in fussy, formal clothing

Domestic – a live-in maid, nanny, cook, etc.

Dragoons – in the British military, soldiers were members of the cavalry

Dysentery – Fever, abdominal pain, and diarrhea called "bloody flux"

Factions – two opposing sides in a dispute, strife, or war

Enfilading – strafing a line of soldiers with continuous gunfire.

Flank – the extreme wings or sides of an army

Hessians – German mercenaries or soldiers for hire

Hobble – Using cloth, rope, or leather, the rider loops a circle over the horse's front hoof, twisted into the shape of an '8,' then looped over the other hoof. Hobbling limits the animal's motion.

Howitzers – Cannons that shot long distances

Independence – freedom from outside control; civil liberty

Infantry – military unit carrying rifles, muskets and bayonets

Mount – to climb onto a horse

Musket – a one-shot long gun that the infantry used in the Revolutionary War. The Kentucky/Pennsylvania rifles were superior weapons; few in circulation—each was hand-made, had a better aim, and shot farther with deadly aim because the rifle had a bored barrel.

Palisades – long wooden posts sharpened on both ends stuck in the ground at angles as a barricade

Patriot – a person who fights for his/her country'

Provisions – Food, supplies, equipment, and necessities to wage a war or to take on a journey.

Ramrods – long poles with a rag or sponge to push "cartridges" into the cannon

Repast – To eat food and drink at a meal.

Sect – Like-minded people united for religious, economic, and political reasons

State militia – Soldiers hired to protect their state.

Susquehannock – A Native American Algonquin tribe, originally lived in longhouses in central Pennsylvania. Fought with the British soldiers.

Thumbstock – a leather protector covering the thumb while one of the cannon team blocked the vent hole to avoid sparks shooting out or air being drawn into the bore of the cannon.

Tubers – long, arching, thorny limbs on which raspberries grow

Turnpike – a road with a toll charge or payment for use of that road.

Tallow – candles made from animal fat

Tory – a political party supporting the British cause during the Revolution. Often called Loyalists.

Wainscoting – painted wood panels running halfway up a wall.

Valise – a soft padded carry-all with handles used as a suitcase

Victuals – food or 'vittles'

Sources

Alexander, Kerri. "Mary Ludwig Hays (1754-1832)" at National Women's History Museum. Museum viewed at: https://www.womenshistory.org/education-resources/biographies/mary-ludwig-hays.

Bell, Richard. *The Great Courses: Ordinary Americans in the Revolution.* College Park, Md.: University of Maryland, 2003.

Bearce, Stephanie. *The American Revolution: Spies, Secret Missions, and Hidden Facts.* Waco, Texas: Prufrock Press, 2015.

Bertanzetti, Eileen Dun. *Molly Pitcher, Heroine.* New York: Chelsea House Publishers, 2002.

Bobrick, Benson. *Angel in the Whirlwind: The Triumph of the American Revolution.* New York: Penguin Putnam Inc., 1997.

Bohrer, Melissa Lukeman. *Glory, Passion, and Principle: The Story of Eight Remarkable Women at the Core of the Revolution.* New York: Atria Books, 2003.

Bone, Beverly. *Images of America.* Mount Pleasant, S.C.: Arcadia Publishing, 2020.

Civic Club of Carlisle. *Carlisle Old and New. I-IV.* Harrisburg, Pa.: J. Horace McFarland Co., 1907.

"Dr. William Irvine" viewed at www.irvineclan.com.

Drury, Bob and Tom Calvin. *The Heart of Everything That Is Valley Forge.* New York: Simon and Schuster, 2018.

Ealer, Joe, director. *The Men Who Built America: Frontiersmen* viewed at The History Channel on February 6, 2023.

Eaton, Jennifer. "Two Faces of Molly Pitcher," *Pennsylvania Heritage Magazine*, Spring 2022, Volume XLVIII, Number 2.

Franklin, Benjamin. *The Autobiography of Benjamin Franklin. 2nd ed.* New York: Bedford/Martin, 2003.

"General Charles Lee" viewed at https://www.Revolutionary-War.net>generalcharleslee.

"General 'Mad' Anthony Wayne" viewed at www.battlefields> VallleyForge>.

"General Nathanael Greene" viewed at www.battlefields> VallleyForge>.

Landis, John. *A Short History of Molly Pitcher, the Heroine of the Battle of Monmouth.* Carlisle, Pa.: The Corman Print Co., 1905.

Levy, Joe. *Really Useful: The Origins of Everyday Things.* New York: Firefly Books Ltd., 2002.

Meyer, Holly. *Belonging to the Army: Camp Followers and Community During the American Revolution.* Columbia, S.C.: University of South Carolina Press, 1996.

"Molly Pitcher" viewed at the U.S. Field Artillery Association: https://www.fieldartillery.org/story-of-molly -pitcher.

"Molly Pitcher" viewed at the Cumberland County Historical Society: www.cumberlandcountyhistoricalsociety.com.

Morrisey, Branden. *Monmouth Courthouse 1778: The Last Great Battle of the North.* New York: Osprey Publishing, 2004.

"Nathanael Greene" viewed at https://georgiaencyclopedia.org>.

Paine, Thomas. "The Crisis" viewed at https://www.us
history.org/paine/crisis/c-01.htm.

Reader's Digest, ed. *America's Fascinating Indian Heritage:*
The First Americans: Their Customs, Art, History and
How They Lived, Pleasantville, NY: Reader's Digest,
1995.

Ridner, Judith. *A Town In-Between: Carlisle, Pennsylvania,*
and the Mid-Atlantic Interior. Philadelphia: University
of Pennsylvania Press, 2010.

Taylor, Alan. *American Revolutions: A Continental History,*
1750-1804. W.W. Norton and Co. 2016.

Thompson, D.W. and Merri Lou Schaumann. "Goodbye
Molly Pitcher," *Cumberland County History,* 1989
Summer, Volume 6, Number 1.

Turn: Washington's Spies (TV Series 2014-2017)—
IMDb. Season 1. https:www.tvguide.com/turn-wash-
ington
-spies/cs1030570354

Ward, Emily Leigh. *Ladylike: The Necessity and Neglect*
of Camp Followers in the Continental Army. Thesis at
Western Kentucky University, 2021.

Wood, Gordon. *The American Revolution, A History.* New
York: Modern Library, 2003.

Zambone, Albert. "Daniel Morgan: A Revolutionary Life"
episode on *American History,* C-SPAN3, viewed May
6, 2019.

Acknowledgments

Any story takes many eyes and hands to transform words into a book, but history requires researching the facts to render the people, the conflict, and the story accurate. Therefore, I thank Sunbury Press, especially my editor, Lawrence Knorr, and the Charles Bruce Foundation, for the privilege of portraying Mary Ludwig Hays McCauley as the heroine of The Monmouth Courthouse on June 28, 1778. Thanks also to my writing team—Sherry Knowlton, Pat LaMarche, Phyllis Orenyo, and Andy Carey—for their corrections, insights, and suggestions for improving this book. I owe Melissa and her husband, Colonel (retired) Thomas E. Shepherd, Artillery Field Officer and former Army War College instructor, a titanic thanks for saving me a major faux pas regarding black gunpowder, loading, and care of cannons during battles. As always, I want to thank my sons for their computer expertise, positive reinforcement of my efforts, and my husband's aid with historical details

I'm indebted to Kim Laidler, manager of the CCHS History on High Shop, and PJ Heyman, owner of the Village Artisans Gallery and Studios in Boiling Springs, Pennsylvania. Thanks to the Cumberland County Historical Society for the information on Hays-McCauley's memorial. And thanks to Alida Hodgson for her designs and long-standing friendship. As always, thanks to Crystal Devine for the magic she performs in preparing the manuscript for printing.

When I found conflicting accounts in my research, I noted them. For example, the numbers of Continentals and British: One text stated that General Washington had 11,000 men at Valley Forge; another said 14,000. Yet another states that causalities varied at the Battle of Monmouth, from several to three hundred plus.

I've used words that reveal the tone, language, and description of the 1700s for realism; readers may not be familiar with specific terms; therefore, I included a glossary of archaic words in the book.

Finally, the TV series *Turn* and *Outlander* offered valuable visuals regarding uniforms, colonial dress, the use of spies, ciphers, behavior, décor, etc. I recommend watching both series for context to the content in *Carlisle's Molly Pitcher.*

Readers and writers have responded positively to my debut history book, *Madam Bessie Jones, her life and times,* so I hope they express similar sentiments about *Carlisle's "Molly Pitcher."* I would also appreciate a review posted on Amazon and Goodreads! I wish the same for my Carlisle Crime Cases, which include *Dying for Vengeance, Courting Doubt and Darkness, Darkness at First Light, Had a Dying Fall,* and *Things Strangled.*

The Internet helped with McCauley's history—rather her story. And to my late sister, I offer thanks for the links she sent about other women like Deborah Sampson and Margaret Corbin, who fought in this war. May some author tell all their stories.

About the Author

J. M. West is the author of the award-winning *Madam Bessie Jones, Her Life and Times*, a tapestry of the history of a local brothel owner's struggles and sacrifices to survive. *Carlisle's Molly Pitcher* is her second local history book. West also penned the fact-based Carlisle Crime Cases featuring homicide detectives Christopher Snow and Erin McCoy, including *Dying for Vengeance*, *Courting Doubt and Darkness*, *Darkness at First Light*, *Had a Dying Fall*, and *Things Strangled*. Her debut novel, *Glory in the Flower*, depicts four coeds' struggles during the turbulent sixties.

West is a Professor Emerita of English Studies at Harrisburg Area Community College, The Gettysburg Campus. She also taught at Messiah College and Shippensburg University and served as Assistant Director of the Learning Center at Shippensburg.

For four years, West co-hosted the *Milford House Mysteries*, author interviews and writing tips on the Bookspeak Network (www.blogtalkradio.com) and volunteered at The Bosler Memorial Library's "The Bookery" for eleven years.

She and her husband live in Carlisle, Pennsylvania. They have two sons and two grandsons. They enjoy their Border Collie mix. In her spare time, West participates in a book club and writing group and reads voraciously.